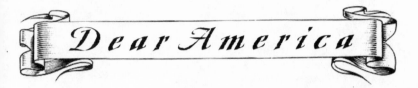

# SEEDS OF HOPE

## THE GOLD RUSH DIARY OF SUSANNA FAIRCHILD

### BY KRISTIANA GREGORY

Scholastic Inc.   New York

# THE *CALIFORNIA*
## 1849

## MONDAY, THE 1ST OF JANUARY, 1849
### ABOARD THE *CALIFORNIA*,
### SOMEWHERE IN THE PACIFIC

We've been at sea now for eighty-seven days. The rolling gray waves spread in every direction as far as I can see. We're still south of the equator, sailing toward the country of Peru. The sun is so warm I carry my parasol when strolling on deck; the thermometer reads 73 degrees.

At this moment I'm sitting in the shade of the mainsail, my dress a hot nuisance around my legs. The barrel next to me is sloshing with only two inches of drinking water. Because of the storms we are two weeks behind schedule and are desperate for fresh meat, water, and vegetables. Many of us are bleeding in our mouths. The voyage around the Horn was rough . . . there was so much loss . . .

Just this morning I finally had the courage to open Mother's trunk. It was in her stateroom, strapped to the wall to keep it from sliding across the floor in heavy seas. When I lifted the lid, a familiar scent of lavender filled me with such longing for her I found myself in tears again.

Still, I wanted to look. On top of her folded nightgown was her journal, the one in which I now write. I flipped through the blank pages. The only thing she had written, in her beautiful script, was the date of our departure from New York Harbor and our names: Dr. and Mrs. Fairchild; Clara, age sixteen; Susanna, age fourteen.

I am Susanna.

## LATE AFTERNOON

Some weeks from now we will land at Fort Vancouver, then travel by wagon to Oregon City where Papa will carry on his medical practice. We have family and dear friends who settled there last year. We are all from Missoura — they traveled overland by wagon and we're going by ship. Papa had long dreamed of an ocean voyage, but we didn't decide on emigrating until after the others were already on the Oregon Trail. Since mail takes so long they won't even know we're coming until they see us walking up their lane.

To finally be with old friends will be a great comfort. But who will tell them what happened to Mother? Must I? Or will Papa? He is so distraught he cannot speak of her without turning away. Clara, too.

The sun seems to be lingering over the western horizon, spreading a pink glow. In moments it will slip out of sight, and darkness will be upon us. Already some of the lanterns on deck are being lit. This ends the first day of the New Year and my first entry in this journal. I plan to record the dreams of our family and my own thoughts as well. It is what Mother had intended. These empty pages testify to her sickness the first weeks of our voyage, when she was unable to eat or even hold up her head. Now, so many weeks later, the empty pages speak of our tragedy at sea. I will write of it another time.

## SATURDAY, THE 6TH OF JANUARY

We are still anchored in the sheltered harbor of Callao, Peru. The breeze is as warm as summer. Oh, the pleasure of hearing crickets again, and the croaking of frogs. Other familiar sounds brought me comfort: A dog barked from somewhere in town and there was a church bell at midnight.

On this day three months ago — October 6, 1848 — our family sailed out of New York. Such excitement. Bystanders stood on the pier waving handkerchiefs, shouting "Godspeed!" It was a crisp autumn day; I remember it well. Mother wrapped her shawl around me against the wind as our ship passed the breakwater and hit open sea. The Atlantic Ocean that day was green and calm. Clara and Papa explored the deck arm in arm. Our grand adventure was beginning.

Our vessel, the *California,* is a side-wheeler steamship, heading for what is to be her home port of Panama City. From there she will sail up and down the Pacific coast delivering and picking up mail. That is why most of her cabins are empty at this time. Not counting the crew there are only a few of us aboard, though there is room for about 200 passengers.

Captain Forbes says we are making history because we will be the first American steamer to sail from the east coast to the west coast.

A curious sight aboard ship is the Tar Heads. This is my name for the sailors who paint their hair with tar to keep it from blowing in their faces. Last night I watched one of them dance to the music of a squeezebox . . . his pigtail bounced on his shoulders like a black stick.


## TUESDAY, THE 9TH OF JANUARY

Once again we're at sea.

About seventy new passengers, mostly men, came aboard at Callao and are unpacking their bags in the empty cabins. For some reason these Peruvians — every one of them — are in a rush for California. Their language is Spanish but some know a little English, though it is hard to understand their accents. When Papa heard the word "gold," he looked at Captain Forbes.

*What is this about gold?* they said to each other.

For supper Cook is serving fresh chicken, potatoes, and one whole onion per person, to eat like an apple. Papa says the vitamins will help our scurvy and keep us from losing teeth. This scurvy is a horrible disease. It has made our gums swell and bleed because we've been so long without vegetables or fruit. We eat at the captain's table, under the skylight. That is why Clara is handing me a clean apron to tie around my soiled dress . . . I confess that one of the things I most look forward to about Oregon is being able to do a proper laundry and to soak in a proper bath.

Most of all, Clara and I yearn to be reunited with friends who knew Mother — Aunt Augusta and Uncle Charles especially, and our cousins.

## WEDNESDAY, THE 10TH OF JANUARY

Sunshine lit our porthole early this morning. It is now 6:30; breakfast will be at seven bells. I am dressed, my face washed, and my braid is tied with a blue ribbon. I am ready to face the day but Clara is still barefooted and struggling into her corset! With so many men on board she wants to look like a lady. I told her it is enough that she combs her hair atop her head and wears her tiny pearl earrings. Clara doesn't realize that she is as pretty as our mother and does not need to pinch her waist.

While I wait for her, a breeze comes in through our window. Looking out I can see seagulls diving into the waves after potato peels the cook has thrown overboard. We are not far from land, but Captain

Forbes says it may be another week before we reach Panama City.

Clara and I have been reading *Poems of Ralph Waldo Emerson*, one of the many books and pamphlets Mother packed in her trunk. She knew there would be no school on our long voyage, so she wanted to make sure we could keep our minds active.

I ate only half my onion for it is foul. The fumes made my eyes cry, and its juice stung the sores in my mouth. The rest I will try to eat tomorrow.

## SATURDAY, THE 13TH OF JANUARY

I have made the acquaintance of Rosita Sepúlveda. She is traveling to California with her husband and seven brothers. Her blouse has more bright colors than I have ever seen on one person. It is made from a square of woven cloth with a hole in the center for her head. The rest of the cloth drapes down to her knees. I admire her thick dark braids tied with red string. They hang down her back. She is perhaps twenty years old.

Rosita smiles every time she sees me and speaks in her rapid Spanish mixed with some words of English. Yesterday she invited me into her cabin. From her satchel she unfolded a beautiful length of cloth, the same vivid colors of her blouse. She tenderly arranged it over my shoulders.

Her generosity so touched me there was a lump in my throat as I climbed up to the deck.

## WEDNESDAY, THE 17TH OF JANUARY

Four days since I've written — I must make a better effort. Today was a thrill because once again we are near land.

From the railing of the deck I could see the rounded, lush hills of Panama. Captain Forbes let me raise his spyglass to my eye. I squinted. Shacks and ruined buildings came into view. Chickens and hogs were running through streets with patches of overgrown grass. I had never seen such a shabby town.

As I looked toward the harbor, the view that came into focus startled me. It appeared as if I were inches from a man's face. I twisted the lens to pull back. Several men were looking toward us, dozens of men. I pulled back even more and scanned the length of the beach.

Now I could see hundreds of men, hundreds.

Arms raised. Their mouths were open as if shouting at us, but of course I could not hear them. It seemed they wanted to board our ship.

## THURSDAY, THE 25TH OF JANUARY, PANAMA CITY

At anchor for eight days now. The weather is hot and it has rained nearly every afternoon. Repairs are being made to our vessel, supplies loaded, animal pens restocked. More bunks are being built in the steerage compartment. The mystery why so many men greeted our ship has been solved.

It seems that after we sailed from New York and had been at sea for sixty days the President of the United States, James Polk, announced that gold had been discovered near San Francisco. Word traveled like fire. Soon boats were leaving New Orleans bound for the Caribbean side of the isthmus. By donkey and canoe they traveled across this narrow neck of land to Panama City. Hundreds and hundreds of men did this. They knew our ship was coming 'round the Horn so they waited for us.

These same men are now shouting at Captain

Forbes. Fifteen hundred of them want to buy passage! When told there is room for only two hundred, and when these men saw the dark skin of the Peruvians, bedlam broken out.

"No foreigners!" came the cry. "Americans only!"

Clara and I are huddled in our cabin, afraid to hear the full wrath of the "legal miners," as these men call themselves. Papa keeps coming below to make sure we are all right and to talk to us.

He says the Americans want to drag the Peruvians off the ship! Complaints are that the foreigners are taking up space and if allowed to step on Californian soil, they will be trespassing. Since the gold belongs to the United States they will be thieves, plundering what is not theirs.

I thought of Rosita and her husband and brothers, but I could not think of them as thieves.

## WEDNESDAY, THE 31ST OF JANUARY, PANAMA CITY, STILL

Tomorrow some 250 passengers will be allowed to board . . . all Americans. As there are no piers in this harbor, everyone must get wet wading from the beach to the little boats that will row them out to us. Papa said many will pay one thousand dollars for the privilege.

Before dinner I went through Mother's trunk again — oh, everything I touched brought the memory of her to me. A brooch she had worn our first day at sea was in a small box with her other jewelry. Clara agreed I could give the pin to Rosita.

Our new friend was overjoyed. She fastened it to her blouse by her shoulder, and said to us in English, "Thank you, lady friends."

## THURSDAY, 1ST OF FEBRUARY, 1849
## AT SEA

At 8:45 this morning we weighed anchor and steamed away from Panama. Captain Forbes decided he would not force the Peruvians to get off the ship, but they must haul all their gear topside. They are to sleep on deck, in hammocks or beds of their own making. Foul weather or fair. I told Rosita she may sleep with us, but the captain overheard us talking. He said no.

"Cabins and steerage are for Americans only."

The *California* now has approximately 400 people on board, weighing our decks down a little lower in the water. If Captain Forbes is worried about her sinking, he is keeping it to himself.

Clara and I brought supper down to our cabin. She is now reading by the swinging lamplight. In these hours alone in our cabin I find myself missing Mother so much it hurts to breathe. To hold her diary in my hands and fill these blank pages with my thoughts is strangely comforting. It is as if she and I are sharing these words. . . .

## NEXT DAY

At dinner Papa was quiet. He folded his napkin under his plate, put his cap on his head, then climbed the companionway without saying anything to us. Clara and I followed him up to the deck. Steam was puffing out of the smokestacks and Tar Heads were coiling ropes after trimming the sails.

"Papa?" I said. "When we get to Oregon, can we plant a garden first thing?"

For so many weeks since Mother's accident, we

hadn't dared breathe any of our hopes or dreams. I don't know why we stopped talking of these things, but now it seemed all right to do so. We were just a couple of weeks away from once again being with loved ones.

Clara and I are now in bed. We have whispered for an hour and still don't understand why Papa is suddenly so quiet.

## WEDNESDAY, THE 28TH OF FEBRUARY, SAN FRANCISCO BAY

Things have not turned out the way my sister and I had planned.

This morning, just when the sun rose behind San Francisco's hills, our ship sailed through the Golden Gate. This narrow channel is perhaps one mile across, with steep cliffs on either side. It opens up to a huge protected bay, the most sensible harbor I've seen in my five-month voyage.

Wood houses and buildings are along the shore, but otherwise the town seems empty. I counted thirty ships of various sizes already at anchor, but oddly most of them had no sailors on board swabbing decks or up in the rigging, as I'm used to seeing in port.

A band welcomed us by playing "Yankee Doodle" and some boys waved at us with American flags. In just 146 days our beautiful little ship sailed from the east coast to the west, the first mail steamer to do so. Captain Forbes stood proudly in the bow, wearing a clean blue coat and cap. He saluted the Stars and Stripes that were snapping in the wind.

Though I'm unhappy to write what happened next, I will, because Mother would have done so. Clara is on her bunk and has started to cry again. I am coming down with a terrible headache.

Here it is: Papa has changed his mind about settling in Oregon! We will get off here, San Francisco, with all our bags and trunks.

"We can't pass up this opportunity," he told us at noon while we were eating our soup. When he explained that he was going to become a miner, Clara and I set down our spoons.

*"What?"* we both said at once.

We are just sick over this. Our own father has gold fever, and Mother isn't here to talk him out of it.

It is ten o'clock in the evening, but there is no one to ring the ship's bell. Besides my family there are just two crew members remaining on board. Two. Captain Forbes and one of the boys from the engine room. That is all.

In the mad rush for shore our captain quickly realized that in addition to the American passengers and the Peruvians, his mates themselves were going ashore. Every single one jumped ship. His navigator, helmsman, first mate, second mate, every Tar Head and cabin boy, even Cook, the firemen, and chief engineer. Everyone.

Our Captain is beyond fury. He held up his hands, pleading with his crew as they hurried away.

"Who will sail my ship?" he cried. I watched him stand there in his crisp uniform, so proud moments earlier. To see a fine captain deserted, mutinied on his own vessel, made me extremely sad. No sheriff or jailer came to help him, for they too have fled to the gold fields. The other ships in harbor have been abandoned as well.

The reason *we* are still on board is that Clara and I told Papa we refuse to leave. Oregon is to be our home, not a mining camp. We want to sail north on the next tide.

"That is what Mama wanted for us," Clara said, "and for us to be close to Aunt Augusta." My sister then broke down crying and would not be consoled. Papa put his hand on her shoulder, but she shrugged it off. When he reached for me, I shook my head and walked away.

## FRIDAY, THE 2ND OF MARCH, STILL ABOARD THE *CALIFORNIA*, SAN FRANCISCO BAY

A cold wind is blowing across the bay, but we are cozy below. I am writing by lamplight at the navigator's table. Last evening was spent without Papa because he went to shore for mining supplies.

Clara and I find ourselves struggling not to cry out of fear and worry. Are we to follow our father or should we go on to Oregon without him? I wish someone could tell us what to do.

Captain Forbes is stricken. He stands on the deck looking out to sea, smoking his pipe. This morning we watched with him as a beautiful three-masted schooner sailed into the bay. As soon as her anchors had splashed into the water, we counted some forty crew members abandoning ship.

"My God," our captain said. "Everyone has the fever."

## SATURDAY, THE 3RD OF MARCH

Papa was in the galley making coffee this morning — we were so happy to see him!

During breakfast our plates nearly slid off the table because heavy swells were rolling the ship. As we ate our salted potatoes, he spoke of everything he'd learned while in the streets and shops of San Francisco.

Gold is easy to find as apples on a tree, he said, trying to convince us to come to the mining camps with him. Just for a few months, he says; a year at most, until he makes enough to buy land in Oregon and build a house. Papa said that as a doctor sometimes he earns just thirty dollars a month, but the men mining gold are pulling in nearly three hundred dollars a *day*.

He lowered his voice and stared into his coffee. "I want to try to recover what was lost."

Papa did not mean Mother, of course, I knew that. Nothing would bring her back to us. He was talking about our life's savings, nearly two thousand dollars.

The memory of how it all happened fills me with such heartache I have put off writing about it . . . but I shall try now to get it out of my mind and onto paper.

Several days after leaving New York we finally recovered from seasickness, except for Mother. She was quite ill. Papa examined her and said it was because she was expecting a baby! We were overjoyed. Gradually she gained strength and by the time we were south of Argentina she was able to walk around her stateroom.

The captain and his navigator decided that instead of sailing around treacherous Cape Horn, they would take a shortcut through the Strait of Magellan. This channel is some 350 miles long and the quickest route from the Atlantic Ocean to the Pacific. We were to learn later that it is also rough with currents and unpredictable winds.

But Mother didn't care. She finally had her sea legs and was feeling so wonderful she wanted fresh air. She took Papa's arm and they strolled on deck,

Clara and I behind them. What happened next came so fast that when I recall it I still can't believe it.

Mother bent over to adjust the hem of her skirt, letting go of Papa's arm as she did. In that instant a wave broke over the bow, sending such a flood of water on deck that we were all swept off our feet. Clara and I grabbed a lifeline that was strung around some barrels; we knew to do this because we'd been at sea many weeks. But Mother had been ill for so long below deck, she didn't know. She threw up her arms in surprise and passed us swiftly in green water that was waist-deep. I reached for her, our hands touched, but she was swept away. The ship rose on a swell and tilted to the side, the gunwale dipping under a wave.

Before our eyes Mother floated overboard. The look on her face was of bewilderment; she called my father's name, then we saw her no more. Papa screamed such a scream I'll never forget. He ripped off his coat to jump in after her, but a sailor caught his arms and wouldn't let him.

The longboat was lowered and two mates began rowing. Our helmsman turned the ship so we could circle, and another mate climbed the mast for a better look. All hands were on deck, trying to help.

Meanwhile, Clara and I clung to each other, clung to the rope. Our dresses were wet and so heavy we couldn't move our legs to stand up. With a growing horror I realized that the weight of Mother's dress would have pulled her under the waves in seconds. The search for her was useless.

I don't remember anything more of that day.

## BEFORE SUPPER

To continue . . . Papa had sewn all our money into the folds and seams of his jacket. He thought that by doing so, no one could steal his life's savings. But it was washed into the sea that day as well. I'm beginning to understand why he wants to dig for gold. It could be the quickest way to earn what was lost, the money part at least.

I feel desolate.

One minute Mother was there, laughing, the next she wasn't. There was no warning, no chance for good-byes, and her watery tomb means we'll never be able to gaze on where she rests. I try to shed this cloak of loneliness, but I cannot. To think about that terrible day brings such heartache.

This is what has brought me to my decision about Oregon. I will talk it over with Clara first, then Papa.

## WEDNESDAY, THE 7TH OF MARCH, STILL ABOARD THE *CALIFORNIA*

In these past days much has happened.

When I told Clara I thought we should go with Papa, her face brightened. She agrees that Mother would want us to stay together. By some miracle we feel hopeful about this adventure. Not until we imagined life without our father did we realize how much we want to be with him.

And so it is. We remain on board, through the kindness of Captain Forbes. He is still trying to muster a crew, and we are saving on a hotel bill. To earn our keep, Clara and I have been cooking the noon and the evening meals. Papa has been rowing to shore with some of the furniture we brought from New York, to barter for the supplies we'll need. Our dining-room chairs, tables, and bureaus brought a few dollars — we don't need those things now.

Papa purchased an assortment of miner's gear: a pan and pick, flannel shirts, a slouch hat, and tall boots; then for our comfort, a canvas tent and a sturdy Dutch oven. We agreed not to sell anything from Mother's trunk. It is small, about knee-high and three feet long, so we'll take it with us. Our tickets for the riverboat cost thirty-two dollars each.

After the breakfast dishes were cleared, Papa spread out one of his maps on the captain's table. Sunshine from the skylight made it easy to read the small print. With his thumb he traced our current position aboard the ship, across the bay, and to a point where a small boat will take us up the winding Sacramento River, some seventy-five miles. At its junction with another river is the town of Sacramento and, nearby, Sutter's Fort. We'll stay there a few days so Papa can hire a wagon to take us up into the hills.

We have been at sea for precisely five months and tomorrow will say farewell. I will miss the fresh, salty air, but not the terrors of the deep.

## MONDAY, THE 12TH OF MARCH, SUTTER'S FORT

In this, our second day at the fort, we've seen nearly two hundred men on their way to mining camps. We recognized Cook and our navigator from the *California*, along with some of the Peruvians. I counted forty-eight Tar Heads who must have jumped ship. One of them told Papa that there are at least fifty abandoned vessels in San Francisco Bay.

I have seen all types of cities in the East, but I've never seen anything like Sutter's Fort. Clara described the people here as "motley," meaning there is every sort of man from every sort of background. Crowds of them are in all stages of departure. Some are camped along the riverbank while waiting for a blacksmith to mend harnesses or wheels. Some are piling their gear onto the backs of mules and are just hurrying away.

Others are bartering their belongings. Clara and I watched one fellow try to sell five thousand ladies' hats he brought with him from New Orleans, which he had hoped to sell at a profit. We laughed because we are the only ladies in sight and we do not need a fancy hat. Another man is trying to unload a case of razors, but there are no buyers because men don't shave their faces around here.

The thick walls of the fort are some fifteen feet high, made of adobe. Within the fort are barracks for soldiers, but we saw no one in uniform. Word is they, too, have abandoned their posts and fled to the hills. There is a bakery, two jails, a carpenter's shop, a grocery, and Captain Sutter's house. His sawmill up the river is where his partner, John Marshall, discovered gold more than a year ago.

Cows and livestock have trampled the surrounding wheat fields and vegetable gardens. There is a bare look to everything. Papa said even the Indians who worked for Captain Sutter have left. Everyone has gold fever.

We've been staying in a room with dirt floors and a pile of straw for our bed. The corners are muddy because we are so close to the water. I should mention that we are now on the American River, not far from Captain Sutter's sawmill. While I'm writing, this page is spotted with fleas! As soon as I brush them off, more hop on — they are terribly irritating. Clara and I are bitten raw about our hands and ankles.

## TUESDAY, THE 13TH OF MARCH

It rained all afternoon. The mud within the walls of the fort was so sticky it pulled off my shoe as I stepped around the campfire. Never mind, for at supper there was great excitement.

A group of men came down from the hills to get provisions — they are originally from Oregon Territory! After talking to them Papa learned that in the past few months some *three thousand* men have journeyed here from that northern territory. In fact, his dearest old friend, Jesse Blue, is nearby at Miner's Creek.

I watched Papa's face when he heard this report. He ran his fingers through his beard and smiled in a way we have not seen him smile since Mother died. It seemed he stood taller, such was his relief that a loyal friend was so near. I admit feeling hopeful myself, but perhaps not for the same reason.

Mother and Mrs. Blue were next-door neighbors all their growing-up years and were dear friends. Our families shared Christmas and birthdays for as long as I can remember. Mr. Blue is like an uncle to me. To look at him will be to look at someone who has heard the voice and seen the smile of my beloved mother.

Maybe the mining camp won't be so lonely after all.

When the Oregon men finish getting their supplies together, they will guide us along the North Fork to their camp where Mr. Blue and possibly more of our friends are mining. When they unrolled a map by the light of our campfire, I was equally relieved that we wouldn't be traveling alone.

There are at least six places called Miner's Creek!

And to confuse things further, four places are named Angel's Camp, several are Dead Man's Gulch, same for Whiskey Town, Gouge Eye, Rough and Ready, Murderer's Bar, Poverty Bay, Old Dry Diggings, Hang Town, and so on. Papa marveled at so many duplicate names, wondering aloud how folks would ever find one another. But my eyes grew wide at the words themselves: poverty, murderer, dead man, hang town. . . . Clara and I looked at each other, and I could see that the deep breath she drew was as shaky as mine.

What is Papa getting us into? In my quiet moments I wonder if he worries, as I do, about his new profession. How will a man trained in medicine know what to do with a pick and shovel?

Because my sister and I are the only females at the fort, Papa watches us carefully, making sure that

men who stare at us keep their distance. He is nervous for our safety because many of these miners are
ne'er-do-wells, that is, thieves, murderers, and pick-
pockets who are hiding from the law.

P.S. At the store I found a little book called *A
Christmas Carol* by Charles Dickens. Before bed
Clara and I take turns reading aloud, then Papa
reads to us. Even though it is long past Christmas,
we are still enjoying the story. So far it's about Mr.
Scrooge, a greedy man with money but no friends.

A lantern set on the floor casts long shadows up
the wall. Clara wants me to hurry this so we can
blow out the light and crawl into our bed of hay. She
and I have returned to a childhood habit that com-
forts us. Before we fall asleep, we pull the blanket
over our heads and whisper our prayers.

## FRIDAY, THE 23RD OF MARCH, MINER'S CREEK

Well, here we are.

From Sutter's Fort we followed the American River
to its North Fork. For one solid day our trail took us

past many rivulets of white water that poured down from the hills, most of which our mules and wagon crossed without getting too wet. At last our guides led us along a wide shallow river with sandbars curving out from the beach.

White canvas tents are planted along the shore and hillsides, dotted everywhere like wild mushrooms. Men stand knee-deep in the river, bending over their pans. Others dig with shovels, some are swinging picks to break apart rocks. Papa said this is called placer mining, when dirt is washed with water to find gold.

As we drove into the settlement, someone looked up and shouted, "Wimmin!"

Every head turned our way and stared as if they had never seen two girls in sunbonnets before. Some fellows lay down their tools and approached us, removing their hats respectfully. When they wouldn't stop looking at us, Papa tipped his own hat to them.

"Gentlemen," he said, "get about your business." Then he snapped his reins until our mules pulled the wagon forward.

The town of Miner's Creek sits in a clearing at the lower end of a meadow. It does not look like a town. It is just rows of shacks and dirty tents facing one another with planks of wood sticking out the front doors like tongues. These walkways are so people don't lose their shoes in the deep, sticky mud. There are several saloons and stores, a blacksmith, and a hotel. A lady in front of the dance hall was watching men go by. Her dress was satin, her cheeks and lips were painted red. Papa wouldn't look at her, and he told us to never go near that place.

Our new "home" is on the sunny side of the creek, on a wide flat ledge of dirt. If the river rises we will stay dry. And when the sun moves across the sky, our tent will be bathed in warm light instead of the shadow of a mountain. Because the elevation here is nearly one mile above sea level, the air is cold and the shade even colder.

When Papa drove in the last stakes, he brushed his hands against his pants and said he was going to look for his old friend, Jesse Blue.

## NEXT DAY

Early this morning I woke to a new sound: hammers and picks striking rock, rhythmically, like the ticking of a tin clock. Miners are everywhere along the river.

For breakfast I fried thick slices of ham in our skillet. Our campfire sits in front of our tent, then beyond us about twenty feet is the river. Clara fetched water in our pail so we could boil potatoes. Apparently we are camped on what used to be a grove of little pine trees. They were chopped down, leaving stumps of various heights, some tall enough to use as a table, others low enough for stools. This is where we were sitting when a great commotion broke out, an hour after sunrise.

"Gold!" someone yelled above the noise of the river. "Mile north of Old Dry Crik!"

Suddenly the noise of picks and shovels stopped. Before our eyes a swarm of men hurried out of camp to where their horses were grazing. They mounted, then disappeared into the woods. Others packed tools and bedrolls onto their mules; some just started walking.

I was amazed at the power of that one word, *gold*.

"Where'd everyone go?" Papa asked as he emerged from the tent. He was rolling up his sleeves and squinting across the brightness of the river.

One of our neighbors is an elderly sea captain. I have never seen such a curious sight as his long, white beard. It has small colorful beads and bells braided into the strands, which make clicking sounds when he moves. He called over from his campfire, "Mister, those boys have gone for better diggings, that's where." Then he waved his hand as if to say good riddance. "There's always something better somewhere. That's gold fever for you."

Papa sat down on one of the stumps. When Clara handed him his coffee, he lifted his cup toward the old sailor. "Say, my friend, have you had breakfast yet? Come on over." And that is how our friendship began with Captain Clinkingbeard. That is his honest-to-God name; I am not making this up.

Meanwhile, there is no sign of Jesse Blue.


## TUESDAY, THE 27TH OF MARCH

Am writing in the tent by lantern light. There is a sweet fragrance of balsam coming from our beds. Papa cut branches from pine trees and spread layers on our cold, dirt floor. With our blankets on top, we have soft beds protected from the frost. Clara is reading; Papa and the Captain are outside in front of the fire trading stories.

About today . . . We learned that to find Jesse

Blue is not as simple as knocking on someone's door. The hills around here are spotted with caves and men hauling rocks out of them. When their luck fails or they hear of a better strike somewhere else, they move on. That's why a fellow's tent might be here one day, gone the next. Also, there are creeks, streams, rivulets, and waterfalls — so many places a man can pan for gold.

Papa walked around for a few hours that first afternoon looking for our friend, but soon realized the search could take longer. When he said he wanted to post a message in town, I tore out a blank page from this journal and gave him my pencil.

We went with him to the Mad Mule Saloon. Letters and advertisements were tacked up outside all over the front wall. Papa pushed his note onto a nail and said if Jesse sees this he'll know where to find us.

## WEDNESDAY, THE 28TH OF MARCH

This afternoon Papa started his new occupation, mining for gold. I do not think he knows what he is doing.

First, he and the Captain had a long conversation

around our campfire, enjoying each other's company while Clara poured them cup after cup of hot coffee. I fried flapjacks. They burned around the edges because I am not used to cooking out in the open — the wind makes the fire too hot. Anyway, when the sun was nearly overhead, Papa turned his pipe upside down and tapped the ashes out against a rock; the Captain did the same.

"Well!" they said, then off they went with shovels and picks over their shoulders. They didn't work near our cabin because the shore is already crowded with miners.

Meanwhile, Clara and I broke off a pine branch to sweep the dirt from our tent. Then we pulled the blankets off our beds and shook them outside. We took our dishes down to the river to rinse, then left them to dry on one of the larger tree stumps. Tomorrow we will figure a way to wash clothes, but for now we wanted to explore the little town, maybe see if the store had any fresh eggs.

Something we noticed the first day we arrived is that everyone walks with his head down! I wondered, *Why are folks so sad?* But we learned they are not sad; they are on the lookout for gold, all the time, every day, hoping to stumble on a nugget that has washed down from the hills. Last week a man found one the size of a yellow apple, right behind the Bliss Hotel. A rainstorm had loosened the earth, and people were finding gold everywhere, in the street and in wagon ruts, even under the plank sidewalks.

This is how it happened that Clara and I bumped into the dance-hall lady — our heads were down. We were courteous to her but hurried past the saloon where she was standing. I noticed that her shoes were blue satin.

## BEFORE BED

It is late, almost nine o'clock. Clara and I are outside warming up by the fire. As we look across the river, we can see campfires scattered along the banks and tents glowing with lantern light. Every few minutes we hear the music of guitars rise above the sound of the rushing river. I am sleepy, but before closing these pages will tell about Papa. . . .

He and Captain Clinkingbeard returned at sundown, soaking wet up to their hips. Papa shivered with cold, but he was so excited to show us his day's earnings. He opened up his leather pouch and poured the contents into his palm.

"It's a start," he said. "Maybe a dollar's worth." Clara and I leaned closer. Cantaloupe seeds, that's what the gold looked like, tiny yellow seeds of hope.

Papa was exhausted so we made him sit in front of the fire while I fixed him a plate of stew, and one for the Captain. Clara brought out two dry shirts for them to change into. We spread Papa's wet socks over the stones and propped his boots there, too. As he ate and warmed up, I noticed his pale white feet. He did not complain about standing in icy water all day, nor that his hands were blistered raw.

Suddenly I realized that without our mother here to encourage him, Clara and I must do so. We hurried into the tent and opened her trunk. We found a small brown bottle containing lanolin, scented with cinnamon. After tearing strips of cloth from one of my petticoats, we sat by Papa in front of the fire and soothed this oil into his bleeding palms, then bandaged them. Clara rubbed his shoulders.

When he smiled up at us, my heart melted. I am worried about him. He is not used to such hard work.

The thin leather strap on Papa's money pouch broke, so I made a new one. I braided together some string with one of my old red hair ribbons, then threaded this new strap through the pouch opening. It is sturdy without being too fancy.

## FRIDAY, THE 30TH OF MARCH

Hooray! Clara has given up her corset and packed it away with Mother's things. It hurts her ribs, she said. And she didn't like so many men staring at her womanly figure.

We spent yesterday and today sewing the blue calico Papa bought in San Francisco. Now we each have a loose-fitting dress that hangs from our shoulders. We do not want to look exactly alike, so we made ourselves collars from the torn petticoat; hers is plain white, mine has a laced edge. Clara's sleeves button at the wrist, mine are rolled up to the elbows. She wears a long white apron tied at her waist with a big bow, I wear none. Aprons get in the way. If I need to wipe my hands or my nose, I'll just bend over and use my hem.

In my opinion we look rather plain, but Papa doesn't think so.

When he came into camp after his day of standing in the river, he set his shovel down and opened his arms to hug us. "My beautiful girls," he said.

## MORNING, BEFORE BREAKFAST

Last night the Captain told stories around the fire. My eyes grew wide when we learned he is descended from the English pirate, Old Clinkingbeard, who wove pieces of broken glass into his beard to scare his enemies. The name carried down through six generations of honest sea captains, the seventh being our new friend. But some months ago, when he sailed into San Francisco Bay, his sailors jumped ship, every single one of them. With no money to hire a new crew, he hung a white flag of surrender from the bow of his schooner. Then he himself headed for the hills.

I like Captain Clinkingbeard. When he laughs or rubs his chin, the bells in his beard make a sort of gentle music. I wish Mother could have met him. She admired people who weren't like everyone else.

## MONDAY, THE 2ND OF APRIL

Wash day. If Mother were here, we would boil water in a kettle with soap, then scrub, then boil again for a clean rinse. It would take all day, which means we would have to start before sunrise in order to hang the clothes out long enough to dry. It would be suppertime by the time we folded and put away everything.

Well, since we have no kettle or soap, we just use a shallow eddy of the river. There is a large, wide rock offshore that we can leap onto. From here we bend over the water with Papa's shirts and whatever else is dirty. A few dips and we're done. To dry, we shake things out, then spread them over bushes in the sun. And all this is done before noon, before the sun is overhead.

I forgot to mention that three men were killed last week when the mine they were digging caved in on top of them. Their friends auctioned off their tools and clothes. That is how Papa got his second pair of trousers and blue suspenders; now with his boots and slouch hat he looks quite like a miner.

## FRIDAY, THE 6TH OF APRIL

Yesterday several wagons pulled by mule teams came into town. The rattle of their harnesses and wheels brought most of us out to look. There was great excitement as goods were unloaded, mainly premade buildings that had been shipped in flat bundles from around the Horn. I am now sitting on our rock in the water, writing to the noise of hammers echoing off the hills. Men are putting up new stores and painting signs with bright yellow and red letters. I can see a bakery, a smithy, two hotels, and a grocery that sells fancy goods. There are more tents, too, as every day new gold-seekers arrive. A hoosegow was also built, that is, a jail.

Someone even set up a chicken coop, so soon there will be fresh eggs. The rooster struts through town as if he's the marshal.

## SUNDAY, THE 8TH OF APRIL

A quiet day.

Sunshine warmed our camp early, making it pleasant to be outside without our shawls. After breakfast the Captain leaned against a tree stump to read. Papa sat nearby, smoking his pipe. Despite all the new buildings there still are no churches in Miner's Creek, so we took turns reading from the Bible and sang a few hymns from memory. Even on Sundays we see a lot of men digging or swirling their pans in the river or driving their mules. Many work every day all day long, not stopping until sundown; there's the constant sound of picks striking rock.

Papa says a man should rest his animals and himself one day a week so that they can do well the other six. He doesn't care if these men find more gold than he does or if they will end up richer.

"I don't need a mansion," he said to us at supper. "Just a place where you girls and I can plant a garden."

"Doc, I'm with you," said Captain Clinkingbeard. "No matter how much we have, there's always gonna be some fellow with more. That's the truth."

The four of us have decided to share meals. It is no extra work for Clara and me, just one more spoon and plate to wash, that's all. As Papa sopped up his gravy with a chunk of bread, I noticed his hands are no longer the graceful hands of a surgeon. They are red from the sun and cold water; his blisters have turned to hard scabs. I think he has more courage than I ever will.

Yesterday afternoon we all walked into town to visit the assayer. This is the man who weighs, tests, then buys the gold that men find. His office is a narrow shack between two saloons. He took Papa's pouch and poured the little yellow specks onto his scale. What Papa dug up last week came to five dollars' worth, much less than what he could have earned doctoring. I watched his face for disappointment, but there was none. He smiled enough that his mustache lifted, then he looked at us. "Let's go see about those eggs you wanted."

The store had a basket of straw out front with fresh hen eggs, ten dollars a dozen. Papa looked at the coins in his hand, then went inside. He pointed to a crate sitting on the floor. It was filled with what looked like oranges, but they were blue! A sign said FRESH CORMORANT EGGS, $6 A DOZEN. The man behind the counter said the cormorant is a large sea bird that dives into the waves for fish.

With his earnings Papa bought four of these big blue eggs, some dried figs, and a sack of flour. These things arrived yesterday by stagecoach from San Francisco. This same coach then left this morning with sacks of gold to be minted or deposited into banks.

When we were ready to leave, the storekeeper gave Clara and me each a square of chocolate candy wrapped in waxed paper. Its aroma was so delicious that I ate mine right away, before I was one foot out the door. Not Clara. She tucked hers into her sleeve to save for later. When we were outside, she whispered that ladies are not supposed to gobble up sweets.

I was furious at her all day for saying that.

## WEDNESDAY, THE 11TH OF APRIL

A horrible thing . . .

Early this morning Clara and I went to the river to wash our faces. As we were scooping up the water with our hands something big floated by, just inches from us. It was a man! But he was on his back with dead staring eyes. We were so startled that not until he drifted beyond our reach did we see the knife in his chest. We screamed for Papa.

Now it is evening. Nothing is known about the miner except that he was murdered and his killer hasn't been caught. One of his friends has been showing around the knife, but no one has seen it before.

## MONDAY, THE 16TH OF APRIL

I have been too busy to write. Papa and the Captain are building us a cabin! It has taken three days for them to chop the trees and cut grooves for corners, but now the walls are going up. The door faces the river. Soon we will be warmer at night and safer. Papa wants us to have a door to lock in case he and the Captain must be away overnight. The murderer is still on the loose.

When Clara and I began carrying rocks from the river up to the cabin, we were surprised by some men who wanted to help. I say surprised because they were Peruvians we met aboard the *California*. Their camp is downstream. I asked about Rosita but they didn't understand until I brought out the colorful shawl she had given me. *Oh, yes*, they said, smiling, and pointed toward their camp. I don't know why it makes me so happy to think she is nearby, but it does. I can't wait to visit her.

They helped Papa build our stone chimney and fireplace in just two days. The rocks are stuck together with mud.

This will be our first night to sleep under our own roof, a real roof, since last October.

## WEDNESDAY, THE 18TH OF APRIL

Rain for two solid days. No sooner did Papa and the Captain wedge in the final log overhead and tack down a tarp than the skies opened up. The river is running high and from our open door we see no one standing in the shallows panning. Miners are taking cover in their shacks or in town, going from one saloon to the next. The street is a swamp of mud.

Our cabin is plain, but cozy. A low fire keeps the room warm. We are using Mother's trunk as a table and sitting on the floor when we eat. In the corner by our bed we hung a curtain of canvas made from our tent; this protects us from drafts while we sleep and also allows Clara and me to dress in privacy. Papa has a bunk on the other side of the room. Right now he is playing checkers with the Captain.

Everywhere I look there is something useful.

Shelves near the fireplace hold our flour and eggs, some tins of fruit, and our drinking cups. We are keeping our pans and Dutch oven on the stone hearth, ready for cooking. Papa made hooks for our clothes from deer antlers he found in the woods. His shotgun hangs over the top of the door. For light we have candles and two oil lamps. We have arranged all of Mother's books along the top of the crate.

This morning when I was at the hearth frying bacon I noticed that Papa was looking through Mother's trunk, touching the fabric of her clothes. After some moments he took out his black bag and ran his hands over the leather. I turned toward him, wanting to say something — I don't know what — but he shut the lid and hurried out the door.

He misses Mother, I know it without words. And I think he misses being a doctor.

## NEXT DAY

Happy news! Our old friend Jesse Blue saw Papa's note at the saloon and ran to find us. He was out of breath when he knocked on our door last evening. I almost didn't recognize him because of his full beard and sunburned cheeks. He picked me up by the waist and swung me in a half circle. But when he saw Clara he removed his hat and held it over his heart.

"Such a lady now," he said to her. "Two years since I've seen you last and aren't you the picture of your mother. . . . Where is she?" He looked around, then nodded toward the curtain. "Sleeping?"

There was a moment of pained silence. The whole image of what had happened to Mother played through my memory but I could find no way to explain. Finally Papa cleared his throat.

"Julia went to be with our Lord," he said. Our cabin was so quiet that when a log in the fireplace rolled into the coals, its thump startled us.

Jesse took a deep breath. "Oh, Doc, I'm sorry." Then looking at Clara and me, he swallowed hard as if words were stuck in his throat, but he said nothing.

After he left we went to bed. I stared up at the log ceiling and listened to the crackle of the fire. Somehow, by Papa saying aloud that Mother was gone, it became more real. The loneliness I now felt for her was so sharp. Clara and I lay there for some time, quietly holding hands.

Also, I was thinking about Jesse's trip from

Missoura, across the prairie and deserts. He had loss as well. Clara and I fell silent when he told about his nephews. One died from a rattlesnake bite and two were poisoned after mistaking hemlock for wild carrots. Agonizing deaths, all of them, he said. Soon after this, Jesse and his wife were forced to abandon their wagon with all their belongings when their oxen died. By the time they arrived in Oregon, they had nothing but the clothes on their backs.

"Every treasure we owned is rotting in the middle of some desert," he said. So when he heard that gold was discovered, he headed for California along with hundreds of other men from Oregon.

## FRIDAY, THE 27TH OF APRIL

Nearly one week since I've written.

The placer Papa and the Captain were mining near our cabin has no more gold, so they hiked upstream to find better diggings. They packed a mule with their tools, bedrolls, the Captain's tent, and our shotgun so they'll be able to hunt for food. Papa gave us his money pouch, wrapped tight with the red strap; inside was eighty dollars in silver coins.

"I'll be back as soon as I can." He reminded us to latch the door at night and said he had arranged for some of the shopkeepers to check on us.

The day after they left we woke to a thundering rainstorm and a crack of lightning that was so loud Clara and I bolted up in bed. The walls of our cabin shook as if something had struck it; our tin plates rattled off the shelf down to the floor. Clara threw her shawl over her shoulders and ran to the door; I followed. Rain hit our faces as we peeked outside. A huge pine tree had fallen so close to our cabin, branches were touching it. We tried to push our way outside, but the limbs were heavy and prickly. We were trapped.

"Papa!" we cried. I began to feel panic. Our father was too far away, we knew that, but still we called for him. Would anyone else hear us through the noise of this storm? We left the door open for light and stirred up the fire in our hearth because cold air and rain were coming in.

To console ourselves we baked a little pot of beans with pork and ate them with biscuits saved from the night before. We stared out at the wet tree. It might be hours before anyone would notice what had happened to us. It would take many men with mules to drag the tree away from our door. We had enough food to last a couple of days, but only a small jug of water. It would be empty by evening.

Suddenly I remembered Papa's black bag. I hurried to open Mother's trunk and pulled it out. When I held up the saw, Clara caught her breath. It was a tool Papa used in surgery, to amputate legs, arms, or fingers. Once I watched him cut off a man's broken foot that had turned black with gangrene. The operation was successful, that is, the man lived, but it was horrible to see.

And with this same saw we made a narrow little path from our cabin to the river.

All day long we took turns sawing and peeling away tiny branches. We also took turns drying off in front of the warm fire because the rain chilled us. Finally there was enough space for us to step over the larger limbs and through, like a tunnel. Our arms hurt they were so tired, our hands were scratched and sticky. I don't think we'll ever get the sap out of our dresses. By sunset the storm had softened and men were stumbling out of the saloons. Some of them noticed the fallen tree and came by for a closer look.

"Hello!" we shouted. "We're in here!"

"Well, boys," one of them said, "at least they ain't dead." Then they turned back toward town.

Clara and I looked at each other in disbelief. *How could they just walk away?* Those men made me so mad I leaned out through the tree and yelled at them. Clara pulled me inside and slammed the door.

"Susanna!" she cried. "Don't. It's foolish to make stupid men angry. We must be wise. Papa isn't here to protect us."

I think it's true that mining camps are full of ne'er-do-wells. It seems that as soon these fellows have gold in their pockets they spend it on drink.

## NEXT DAY

We are alone in our little cabin, missing Papa more than ever. This morning we realized this is the first time we've been without both our parents. No friends or family either. Sometimes I feel so lonesome my forehead aches from trying not to cry. I wish we had gone to Oregon after all. Truth be told, I now wish we had never sailed from New York in the first place.

This morning we looked through Mother's trunk

until we found her butterfly net. We took turns holding it in the stream from our washing rock and after an hour caught two speckled trout. Fried up with bacon grease and pepper, they were a delicious breakfast.

## MONDAY, THE 30TH OF APRIL

Last evening after Clara and I were in our night-dresses we heard a man outside, calling our names. We listened hard, trying to recognize the voice, but were afraid to open the door.

We wrapped ourselves in our shawls, blew out the lamp, and waited. When he called again, then he said he was Jesse Blue, we still didn't answer.

Finally Clara lay her cheek against the door and called out, "If you are who you say you are, tell us the childhood name of our mother and where she was born."

The man laughed, then answered correctly: Julia Campbell from Boonesville, Missoura. And he re-membered our pet rooster named Caesar.

We flung open the door and waved Jesse in through the path.

## AFTER BREAKFAST

Jesse stayed until ten o'clock last night, helping us with chores and telling us about Papa. He fetched two pails of water for us and with his axe he chopped wood for our fire. He did not use the branches we'd sawed off because that wood is too green; it wouldn't burn and its sap would make terrible smoke. While he is in town for supplies, he will find some fellows to haul away our tree.

What cheered us up was his news about Papa's claim and his. They are several miles up in the hills and are so close together they can holler to each other back and forth. Our father is well, Jesse said, and working hard. Come nightfall everyone gathers around their campfire to hear Captain Clinkingbeard's stories about pirates.

Clara and I tore paper from this journal and wrote a quick letter to Papa. We folded it, then dripped wax from our candle over the edge. To seal it we pressed a little stone into the wax before it hardened, then handed the letter to Jesse. In exchange he took out a small cloth pouch and gave it to Clara. When we realized he was giving us some of his own gold, we handed it back.

"We'll make do until Papa returns, but thank you kindly."

## BEFORE BED

There has been another murder.

The day Jesse left we walked to town for eggs and dried fruit. Wildflowers are blooming along the sunny parts of the river so we picked a bouquet and put it into an empty bottle we found in the grass. A crowd of men was gathered in front of the hotel. Voices were loud. I started to ask them what they were saying, but Clara held my arm.

She said it is not polite for ladies to approach men without a proper introduction.

I don't know how my sister knows everything, or she thinks she does; she's only sixteen. I am sick of her bossing me around. So when we were in the store I asked the grocer what the fuss was all about. He told us a young blacksmith had been murdered last night behind one of the saloons.

Presently it is eight o'clock and Clara and I are ready for bed. We're glad no one has come to chop away our tree. For all we care, it can block our door until Papa comes home, however long it takes him. It makes us feel safe.

Our bouquet of white, violet, and yellow flowers looks lovely in its "vase." There are so many empty bottles and jars strewn around camp we've begun gathering them. They're all colors: green, red, brown, blue, clear. We've arranged them outside along the western wall of our cabin, poking them upside down into the soft earth. With the afternoon sunlight playing through the glass they are a pretty sight. Other things we found and brought home are an empty cracker tin, a ladder-back chair, and a shovel with most of its handle broken off.

From our leftover calico Clara sewed me a sunbonnet to match my dress. I'm not so mad at her now.

Clara and I are sharing *The Last Days of Pompeii*. She reads at night while I write in my diary; I read in the morning after chores. It's a historical novel set around A.D. 79, very interesting. We discuss it in depth and wish Mother were here to give her opinion as well.

## TUESDAY, THE 1ST OF MAY

After buying groceries we now have sixty-three dollars. We have hidden Papa's money pouch in the tin we found. The tin is wide enough for this journal to fit inside, but flat so it can slip under my pillow.

Caught five trout this afternoon. We fried up two, then hung the others on a string and gave them to our favorite storekeeper. He gave us a nice red onion in exchange.

## BEFORE BED

After breakfast we did our chores quickly, then packed a picnic of buttered bread and figs. As we were leaving, we swept the dirt in front of our cabin so we'd know if anyone tried to get in while we were gone.

For nearly an hour we walked downstream, toward the Peruvian camp. Along the shallows men were squatting in the water, swirling their wide pans with gravel as they searched for gold.

As soon as we came around a bend in the stream, we saw a clearing with several tents and a large fire for cooking. Rosita was standing in the sunshine, hanging shirts on a rope strung between two trees. When we called her name, she set down her basket and ran toward us. Such a happy reunion. We had parted two months ago thinking we would never see one another again.

We were surprised she has learned more English, and also surprised to see that she is going to have a baby!

Her brothers are placer-mining along this fork of the river and up some nearby creeks. Rosita's husband, Tomás, called hello and waved us over to where he stood ankle-deep in the stream. He and another man have built a wooden box about three feet long with ridges in the bottom, like a washboard. One of them shoveled dirt into it, and the other poured water from a pail. All this washed over a smaller box inside that looked like a sieve. They then rocked it back and forth like a cradle to strain out the gold flakes. It is much more complicated than with just a pan, so I asked why they do it this way.

Tomás said that to sit all day in a cold river was to bring an early death.

With sudden alarm I thought of Papa, remembering

how chilled he was after a day in the water. I worry about him getting sick because he's not used to such rough work. The next time Jesse Blue comes into town he must tell us how to find our father so we can hike up to visit him.

Clara and I helped Rosita hang the rest of her wash, then sat with her by the fire where she had buried twenty potatoes in the coals. When we noticed she was using a miner's pan to fry onions, we asked where all her cooking things were, for we'd seen her using pots and a skillet aboard the ship.

"Yankee come and take everything," she said, "and told us go back to Peru." There was no anger in Rosita's brown eyes, just weariness.

There are other foreigners, she said, who have been beaten and robbed of their tools. Chinese especially. She pointed to two of them with shovels, digging into the side of a hill. They wore wide straw hats but did not have the usual braid hanging down their backs.

"Yankee cut their hair off," Rosita said. "To shame those poor boys."

I was upset to hear these things.

At noon we rested by a stream. We shared our figs

with Rosita; she gave us each a roasted potato. When we were thirsty, we leaned over the grassy bank to drink from our cupped hands. Such good, cold water.

We returned home before dark; the dirt in front of our cabin was smooth except for tiny paw prints of rabbits and squirrels. No humans. Clara and I have rekindled our fire, and there's a nice pot of soup simmering on the coals. All the way home we talked of wanting to help Rosita, but we're not sure how.

## NEXT DAY

Pork and beans for breakfast with dried apples. We are out of coffee.

A little burro that lost its mother was wandering through town. This morning when Clara and I saw some boys kicking it, we lifted the hems of our skirts and raced over. This time my sister did not stop me. I picked up some stones and threw them at the boys' feet, not to hurt, but to let them know we meant business. Clara peeled a thin branch from a tree and began whipping their legs until they finally ran from us.

We wrapped our arms around the burro's neck

and spoke softly. It was shaking and it felt bony, as if it hadn't been eating. While Clara stroked behind its ears, I pulled the long blue ribbon out of my braid and tied it around its fuzzy neck. Its head reaches only to my waist; it is that young.

So that is how we came to have a pet. After we led her to the stream to drink, we took her to our camp-site and fed her some oats and a scrambled egg. Then we carved out a thicket from the fallen tree and made a bed of pine boughs. The little thing fell right asleep, her legs curled underneath her small body. During supper we decided to name her Lilly.

## SATURDAY, THE 5TH OF MAY

I am writing by our small oil lamp. Clara is already asleep. Our faces are sunburned because we forgot to wear our bonnets and we were outside all day.

After breakfast we scrubbed the plates in the stream then packed another picnic. We had made a harness and little saddle for Lilly from one of Mother's aprons and some straps of leather. To this saddle we tied on our Dutch oven, our frying pan, and a sack filled with spoons and plates we wanted to give Rosita, and some flour we bought yesterday. We did not bring eggs because we were afraid they would break.

Rosita was thrilled with our gifts but worried we were doing without.

Our family is small, we told her. Rosita has all those brothers and needs more cooking things than we do.

We helped her sweep out the tents and fill her water buckets. Her baby will come at the end of July. She said if only her dear mother had journeyed with her to California, there would be no troubles with the birth.

I told her not to worry, that Papa has delivered hundreds of babies. Clara looked at me as if to say, *But we don't know where he is.*

Will blow out the lamp now. The nights seem so much darker and longer without Papa. He's been gone for just a week, but we wish he would come down from the hills soon.

## MONDAY, THE 7TH OF MAY

This morning Clara and I hurried through our washing chores. With just two of us we have only a few things: aprons, handkerchiefs, and such.

The days are getting warm, though it is still cold

in the shade. Our garden of colored glass grows with each new bottle we find. Now we've made a pretty path down to the river. Lilly grazes nearby and follows us at a trot when we walk into the woods or into town. Those boys don't bother her anymore because Clara carries a switch and I keep pebbles in my pocket. They see us coming and quickly turn around. Some of them work in stores with their fathers, others were cabin boys who jumped ship in San Francisco. I don't know if they are miners or just loafers.

I am writing this outside, on what has become our favorite rock, the one offshore where we fish and wash clothes. Clara is reading a pamphlet of Shakespeare's poems, but I think really she is dozing because her head keeps dropping to her chest. The sunshine makes me sleepy, too, and the splash of the river reminds me of being at sea. Water flows past our rock as if we were on a ship going fast.

## LATER

We saw Jesse Blue this afternoon at the assayer's office, selling his nuggets. Papa loved our letter, he told us, and is still working hard. He and Captain

Clinkingbeard built a Long Tom, which is bigger than the cradle and works even better for sifting gold. Just as I was asking him where exactly Papa's camp was, a fight broke out with gunshots in front of a saloon. There was so much dust and shouting Clara and I hurried away with Lilly.

Now it's time for bed. We still don't know how to reach Papa's camp. Another thing bothers me: The tree blocking our door is beginning to dry out; the pine needles are brown and dropping fast. Clara thinks we need to move it away from the cabin because a spark from our chimney could turn it into a torch.

It is not easy to sleep with worries. I wish Papa were here. We comforted ourselves with sponge baths this evening. The hot water felt wonderful on my face, but we long to have a real soak in a real tub. Before I blow out the lamp, I'm going to start reading one of Mother's favorite books, *Jane Eyre*, by Charlotte Brontë. Clara just finished it.


## TUESDAY, THE 8TH OF MAY

Last night Clara and I awoke to noises that horrified us. We sat up in bed, straining to see through the dark cabin. I was afraid to breathe. It sounded as if someone was outside, pushing his way through the tree to our door.

We crept across the cold floor to look out through a crack between logs. Darkness was all we saw. I wished we had Papa's gun or the frying pan we had just given to Rosita.

We could hear the snap of small branches being stepped on and the rustling of larger ones being pushed aside. My heart raced with fear. There was a sound of someone or something breathing heavily, and there was a terrible stink. Not like whiskey, but an odor like rotting cheese.

I felt so alone standing there in my nightdress and bare feet, too afraid to even whisper. My sister and I clung to each other, waiting. We listened to the footsteps slowly circle our cabin, then pace along the wall of our chimney. At long last, the noise faded away into the woods. When we thought it was safe, Clara lit a candle so we could look outside for our little burro. Lilly was in her nest, awake but shivering, protected by the tree's thick branches.

After breakfast we went together to fill our bucket and to wash dishes. That's when we saw the prints in the soft dirt. They were from some animal, huge ones, bigger than my own hand spread out. A miner standing in the river answered our call to please come look.

"Grizzly," he said.


It is windy tonight and the air smells like rain. Clara and I are ready for bed. We have latched the door and rolled heavy stones in front of it. A low fire is burning in the hearth in case we need to make a torch. The miner told us that flames are about the only thing that will scare away a grizzly.


## SUNDAY, THE 13TH OF MAY

We are worried about the bear, but more worried about our dry tree catching fire. So on Tuesday we asked one of the storekeepers if he could find some men willing to help us drag the tree away. He came to our cabin that evening with two hatchets and a ball of twine, then apologized that no one else was willing to help.

Never mind. Clara and I have been chopping branches all week. We gathered bundles, tied them with string, then hooked them onto Lilly's harness. Every couple of hours we rested from our woodcutting by walking with our pet a short distance from camp to dump the wood. If there's a forest fire everything will burn, but at least we won't be trapped in our cabin.

The long tree trunk is still there, but with the branches gone we were able to roll it a few yards away. It is quite heavy. Every day we listen and look out for the bear.

Papa's been gone two weeks.

## MONDAY, THE 14TH OF MAY

It took longer to do wash this morning because our calicoes were so dirty. But while things were drying in the sun, Clara and I put on our traveling dresses from our sea voyage and walked with our burro to visit Rosita. When she heard about our tree, she called to her husband in Spanish. Within an hour he and four of her brothers had axes over their shoulders and were escorting us back to our camp.

From the tree trunk the men cut four pieces and brought them inside for us to use as stools. Then from the thickest part of the trunk they cut a piece that stands about two and a half feet high. They rolled it into the middle of our room and settled it with its flat side up — so now we have a round table.

Clara found a pretty white cloth among Mother's things, which we have spread over our new table. In the center is a tin can filled with wild red roses we picked from along the river. The room is most homey. We wish Papa were here to enjoy it with us. Clara and I find ourselves talking more and more about our mother, and without tears. *She would love these flowers. . . . Mother would be pleased with the way we keep house. . . .*

I almost forgot — Rosita gave us a straw hat she found floating down the river. With her help we cut two holes in the top and fit it over Lilly's tall ears. Then we tucked some wild daisies into the crown. Just looking at our dressed-up donkey we laugh and feel hopeful.

## NEXT DAY

Our flour and sugar are low so after chores we will go into town. First, to tell how we cooked our eggs this morning.

The shovel we found is made of stiff metal. We

washed it in the river, scraping away the dirt with our penknives — our fingers were numb from the cold water after this! Clara set the shovel in our fireplace to heat over the coals; its broken handle is just long enough for us to grab without burning ourselves. I rubbed bacon grease over the surface, which curves up like a skillet, and then when the grease sizzled, Clara cracked in seven eggs. They fried up nice and golden. We ate them with biscuits and dried apricots.

Just fifty-six dollars in Papa's money pouch. We hope he returns soon.

## THURSDAY, THE 17TH OF MAY

This was the worst day in Miner's Creek.

After breakfast Clara and I were down by the stream cleaning the shovel and our plates. We could see into town. When we noticed that Jesse Blue was walking out of the new bakery, my sister and I looked at each other.

*Why does he come into town so much, but Papa doesn't?*

We quickly put away our utensils and tied on our

bonnets and clean aprons. As we marched toward town our little burro followed us, braying with concern. In front of the assayer's we adjusted her hat and told her everything was going to be all right. I don't know if she understood us, but she is as loyal as a dog — we don't have to tie her up.

Jesse Blue was inside. He smiled when he saw us and held out a small pouch. "Take it, it's from your father. One solid ounce."

Clara opened it and poured the golden flakes into her palm, about a teaspoon's worth.

An ounce is worth sixteen dollars. I thought to myself that Papa has been gone for three weeks and he is working awfully hard to make so little money. I didn't thank Jesse because there was only one thing on my mind.

"Draw us a map so we can find Papa's camp." I expected Clara to scold me with her eyes for not saying "please," but her gaze was also on Jesse.

He promised he would come by this afternoon with a map, but it is presently 8:30 in the evening and Jesse Blue is nowhere in sight. One minute we are furious at him for breaking a promise, the next we are worried that something may have happened to Papa's old friend.

There's something worse, though.

After supper, when I reached under my pillow to pull out our tin, I noticed the lid was on crooked. Carefully I opened it to take out my diary. My breath caught in my throat.

Papa's pouch was gone.

Clara and I are distraught that a thief came into our cabin while we were away. Nothing else seems to be missing, but we are still upset. What I didn't tell her is how angry I am that a stranger may have read these pages, my intimate thoughts and feelings.

Mother would not approve of this, but we now bring Lilly into the cabin every night. I don't know why the grizzly didn't eat her that night, but we're not taking any chances. We've made a soft bed for her from the hay the storekeeper brought us, and hung up her hat. She sleeps in front of the door. If anyone tries to get in, he will bump into Lilly and she will not be happy. When our burro is mad or worried, she brays so loud she sounds like a goose. Her cry will wake us and, we *hope*, scare away the intruder.

On the subject of thieves, the murderer has not been caught.

## FRIDAY, THE 18TH OF MAY

We spent today sweeping out the cabin and doing wash. The weather is so pleasantly warm we prefer to be out in the fresh air. Unless our door is propped open, it is gloomy to be inside the cabin. Clara and I want to put in a window, but there is no glass in town for sale and even if there were, we have only Papa's sixteen dollars that Jesse gave to us.

As for reporting the thief, we don't know whom to go to, so have said nothing to anyone.

## BEFORE BED

Lilly is asleep by the door. Clara is kneading bread that will rise overnight on the hearth. We have been talking all evening about what happened earlier. I will write quickly so we can get to bed and talk more.

This afternoon we were in the store buying ginger to bake a spice cake. A man leaned against the counter talking to the owner as if they were good friends. This man glanced at me, then feasted his eyes on Clara, with a slow grin. His teeth were brown with tobacco juice that ran down into his beard.

Horse manure coated the man's boots and his pants were soiled with grease.

Clara turned to me and whispered, "Susanna, let's go."

I placed a nickel on the counter for our little sack of ginger, then met her by the door. As I nodded good-bye to our grocer friend, I noticed something that put chills up my spine.

The man was paying for a plug of tobacco with coins he pulled from a leather pouch. There was no mistaking the braided red strap that I had made for Papa.

Clara had seen it, too, because she squeezed my arm. How I wanted to kick that thief and grab away Papa's pouch, but remembered Clara's words: *We must be wise.* So we quickly left.

Once home we brought Lilly in and rolled more rocks against the door. There was something other than the man's filth that scared us. His eyes were cold. We worry because he knows our cabin and probably knows we're alone. But we don't think he knows that *we* know who he is. He seemed too stupid and dirty to realize that the pouch he stole is unique and could easily be claimed by its owner, our father.

Meanwhile, we will keep this to ourselves. We are more anxious than ever for Papa to return.

Clara has finished with the dough and placed a damp cloth over the bowl. By morning it should be a tall, soft loaf ready to bake. Off to bed now and more talk . . . we are too nervous to sleep. Our poor little burro has no idea how much we are counting on her.

## MONDAY, THE 21ST OF MAY

A new development. It is late, nearly midnight. I am writing quickly while Clara wraps some food and blankets for Lilly's pack. We'll leave tomorrow at first light.

While we were sitting by the stream this morning, a miner rushed into our campsite. He was covered with black soot and was crying out for Dr. Fairchild.

Before we could explain about Papa, two men carrying a stretcher came into view. On it was a boy about Clara's age, moaning with pain. His face was bloodied and he was breathing hard. When the men pulled back the blanket and I saw a broken bone sticking out above his ankle, my thought was only of myself: *I will die before I use Papa's saw to do surgery.*

I soaked my handkerchief in the river and gave it

to my sister. As she kneeled over the boy to wash his face, she asked the men what had happened.

They said there was an explosion in a mine up-river. The fuse was short so the black powder exploded too soon. Three boys were killed right away, but Sam was rescued from underneath some rocks. The men demanded to see the doctor.

"He's not here," I said. Clara and I were examining the boy's neck and face, his shoulders and arms, touching gently. We'd seen Papa do this, work his way down the body, searching for injuries. When we came to his ribs, he screamed.

Clara pointed to his chest, where she had felt a broken rib. "If he moves, it will puncture his lung," she said. "We have to wrap him so he'll stay still."

I hurried into the cabin to find cloth to use as bandages, but as I opened Mother's trunk something better came to mind.

Clara's corset.

We cut away Sam's shirt, then gently slipped the corset underneath and around him. As Clara laced up the front, our burro came over and stood beside me. Her nose moved as she sniffed the air. The men watched without saying anything.

When we examined the damaged leg, Clara and I glanced at each other.

"We have to get Papa," she whispered.

I nodded.

So that is what we are doing tomorrow. We will follow the river upstream and ask anyone we see about our father. We are praying that God will guide us to him.

Sam is asleep by the fireplace, on a pallet we made. One of the men who carried him is in Papa's bunk and will stay while we're gone. The reason my sister and I are going instead of the men is we want to urge our father to come home for good. No more mining. We need him, and this boy needs him. Rather than one of us staying behind while the other looks for Papa, we're going to be together. Two are braver than one. And safer.

Because the broken bone is exposed to air, Sam is in so much pain he keeps slipping in and out of consciousness. The whiskey his friends poured down his throat numbed him for only a few hours. Clara hunted through Papa's bag and found a bottle of laudanum. We gave the boy a few teaspoons, and he soon fell into a deep sleep . . . no wonder, it's opium mixed with alcohol.

At long last, to bed. I will take this diary with us because I do not want that man to snoop around and find it.

## ON THE TRAIL SOMEWHERE

It is dark except for our fire. Clara and I made camp under a rocky overhang, protected from the wind and wild animals. We are nervous knowing this is grizzly country. I do not like being out here away from our cabin and so far from Papa, wherever he is. At this moment I'm angry with him for leaving us behind. We don't care if he earns back the money he lost at sea. It doesn't matter anymore.

This opening in the rocks is like a wide cave, large enough for us and Lilly to bed down and stay dry if it rains. The only sign that anyone ever camped here is blackened rock overhead, from an old fire perhaps. We are away from the trail, up in a ravine, so we don't think anyone will bother us tonight.

I worry about Sam's broken leg. The wound was

terrible, though we did clean it as best we could with hot water and peppermint leaves. The poor boy begged us to stop, it hurt him so. The bottle of laudanum should last four days.

In a few minutes I'm going to carve Clara's name and mine on the wall, farther in. Then to sleep.

Oh, for supper we boiled potatoes and drank water from the stream. Earlier today some miners told us they didn't know Papa personally, but that there was a fellow everyone calls "Doc" about five miles upstream — we'll head out at first light.

## NEXT DAY

I've lost track of the date, but there are two wonderful things to report.

Sometime after noon we were resting by a quiet little creek and letting Lilly graze when we heard a familiar sound. It was the clinking of tiny bells.

Clara and I jumped up and yelled, "Papa . . . Captain!"

They came through the trees, Papa first. He was so thin, I thought we would crush him when we embraced. We all talked at once. To our delight he agreed immediately to return with us, for the boy's sake, and for ours.

This brings me to our second good thing. I saved it until supper when we were around the fire. Captain Clinkingbeard cooked flapjacks and we ate them rolled up with bacon inside. Good hot coffee, too.

"Papa," I said, "Clara and I found something last night." Reaching into my pocket I pulled out a rock and held it in my palm. It was yellowish, the size of a walnut.

He leaned forward in the light to see better. He put it in his mouth and tapped his teeth against it to make sure it was smooth, not gritty. Even through his beard I could see that his cheeks were hollow and there were dark circles under his eyes. My heart skipped with alarm. He was worn out. When he asked where we had found the rock, I held up my penknife.

"Last night, when I was carving our names." Then I told him about the yellow stripe running through the length of our rocky shelter.

"There's more, Papa." Clara opened up our tin, where I'd been keeping my journal. When Papa saw the gold dust and pebbles, and when he felt how heavy they were, he started to speak, but instead a single tear slipped down his cheek into his beard.

More later.


## Noon, next day

Will write this quickly — we have stopped by a stream for a short rest. Papa and the Captain broke camp before sunrise. Their mule has made friends with our little Lilly. They were nuzzling each other as we loaded their packs.

When we reached our shelter from the night before, Clara and I were flabbergasted to see six men with shovels and picks. We started to march up and tell them to go away, but Papa held us back. He asked if we had staked a claim.

No. Since we were in such a hurry to find Papa we didn't take time to think through everything. We thought if we swept away our tracks and put brush in front of the opening, it would be as we left it when we returned.

The Captain shook his head in sympathy. The ornaments in his long white beard clicked as he rubbed his chin. He called those men "opportunists," said they must have been watching us from afar then moved in after we left.

Clara's face was red as she struggled not to cry. "It's not fair," she said.

"No, it's not," said Papa. "But life's not fair."

As we walked he explained how easy it is to make a claim. All we needed to have done was write our names on a piece of paper, tack it up in front of our spot, then hammer some stakes into the ground marking it off. Or sometimes a person just leaves his tools there to say the place is his. That's it.

I burst into tears, embarrassed by our costly mistake. My misery reminded me of the filthy man who had broken into our cabin so I told Papa about that as well.

He put his hand on my shoulder. "It's my fault for not teaching you girls to file a claim and I never should have left you alone for so long, I'm sorry. As for the thief, a dangerous man is best left alone, especially with no sheriff to enforce the law." Papa said that some injustices we must leave up to God to make right.

><

# HOME AGAIN

Finally, after a month of being apart, our family is under one roof again. Clara and I are so relieved. Papa may not be able to fight off a grizzly, but we know he will keep us safe from terrible men.

Captain Clinkingbeard put up his tent outside next to our wall so he'll be more protected from the weather.

The splint Clara and I made for Sam's leg held together, though the skin around the wound is bright red, spreading in green streaks up toward his knee. It smells bad. The man watching over him for four days kept Sam bathed, but still the room stinks of urine and rotting meat.

Sam was hot with fever. His lips were dry and bled a little as he tried to talk to Papa. "Please . . ." was the only word we heard.

I heated a pot of water so we could all wash our hands. When Papa opened his bag, he looked at his saw through squinted eyes, then looked at us. In whispers we explained about the fallen tree. Sam's friend has hurried the saw to a blacksmith's to have it sharpened. Now we wait.

Sam is sleeping again. Meanwhile, there is enough hot water for Papa to take a sponge bath behind our

curtain. Clara has laid out a clean shirt and dunga-
rees for him.

I am cooking potato soup in a small kettle we found
off the trail, but I don't feel like eating. The thought
of what awaits poor Sam makes me feel sick inside.

## WEDNESDAY, THE 30TH OF MAY

Days are hot now. The ground outside our cabin is
carpeted with pine needles that smell wonderful from
the sun. We keep the door open all day for fresh air,
though doing so lets in flies that swarm in the center
of the room.

About Sam. The night we returned, Papa readied
him for surgery, near 11:30. His pallet was raised
onto the log stools to make it easier for Papa to work.
We lit all the candles and lamps, putting them high
on shelves and hanging from beams to cast the
brightest light. Clara and I prayed with the boy and
gave him a good swig of laudanum. He was panicky.

"Don't take my leg, Doc," he pleaded. Papa didn't
answer. The infection was deep, and there was no
way to repair the bone, not in a mining camp anyway.

Clara knelt on the floor and held Sam's head with

her cheek against his, to comfort him. Because of his broken ribs I could not drape myself over his chest to hold him down. Instead, we strapped his hips to the cot; his friend held one arm, I held the other. I watched Papa's face. There was kindness in his eyes and a calm determination to save Sam's life. I felt such love for my father and relief that he was home again.

But suddenly my courage failed and I turned away. As the boy struggled under Papa's saw, I began to cry.

Then it was over.

Later . . . Papa's clean shirt was spattered with blood. So were the bed and floor. We all worked quickly through the night, first caring for Sam, then spreading buckets of clean dirt on the floor. Clara and I took the soiled blankets and clothes to our washing rock, and under the light of a half moon we rinsed everything out. The friend dug a hole beyond the cabin to bury the damaged leg, then piled rocks on top to keep animals away. We took turns watching Sam until dawn.

Presently Papa and Clara are at the assayer's, having our gold tested and weighed. I have been so tired I forgot to ask about Jesse Blue, if he's all right.

We have a smoky fire in the cabin to keep flies and mosquitoes off Sam. His stump is bandaged with strips of my old petticoat that are changed every few hours. To clean the rags, we dip them in boiling water, then hang them in the sun to dry.

Must go. Sam is whispering my name . . . I think he needs a sip of water.

## FRIDAY, THE 1ST OF JUNE

We have good news. And bad.

First, the good. The gold Clara and I dug out of that cave with our penknives weighed seven pounds, three ounces. Papa made me do the arithmetic. At sixteen dollars an ounce . . . we now have $1,840.

"That's more than you found, Papa," I said when he returned from town, "in all those weeks of standing in the river." I immediately put my hand over my lips, realizing too late that I should not boast, especially when Papa worked so hard. He looked at me, puzzled.

"What do you mean, you found more than I did?"

My mouth went dry as I thought about this question. We were sitting at our table, sunlight coming in through our open door. The only sounds were outside, the squawk of a blue jay and a squirrel chittering.

Now the bad news.

Papa explained how he sent Jesse Blue to town several times, to give us the gold he had mined. He didn't know exactly how much each sack weighed, but he figured each was as heavy as a frying pan. A few pounds, he knew, probably worth four thousand dollars total. Since Jesse's own claim had run dry and he was penniless, Papa told him he could have five ounces of dust for himself, each time he went to the assayer. Clara and I were speechless. For all of our father's hard work she and I were given just one ounce.

Papa stared out the door, shaking his head.

Clara burst into tears. "It's not fair. . . . I hate gold! It makes people greedy and do bad things."

I was too furious to cry and was full of questions. Did they have a fight? Did Clara and I do something wrong?

Nothing like that, he said. They were friends. Jesse Blue loved us as daughters.

"Then why did he steal from us?" Clara cried.

Papa put his head in his hands. Some moments later he said, "I guess the temptation was too much."

It is late now, almost ten o'clock. Everyone has turned in. I am tired, but too upset to sleep. I must write everything down, but first will give Sam some water and a cool cloth for his head. He is tossing on his cot. He will stay with us so Papa can watch over him until his wound begins to heal. Besides, the cabin he shared with those boys who were killed is no longer his. Several miners moved in and took over. They auctioned off Sam's things because they didn't think he would live.

## MIDNIGHT

Back to Papa. He does not want to speak harsh words against his old friend, but the truth is in front of us. We spent the afternoon in town, asking if anyone had seen Jesse Blue. Maybe there's been a terrible misunderstanding, Papa kept saying to us.

Then all hope was lost. The assayer told us Jesse weighed in with dust worth $4,750 and left on the morning stage for San Francisco.

We are heartbroken.

As Papa lay down in his bunk tonight, he stared up at the ceiling. "Daughters," he said, "I would rather be a poor man with honest friends than a rich man with none." He never dreamed Jesse would think otherwise.

The quiet of this late night helps my mind rest. In a moment I'll blow out the candle.

As for that filthy thief who came into our cabin and stole our coins, I was surely mad. But with Jesse Blue, it's different. He was our friend for so many years, Clara and I looked up to him. He knew our mother; she loved him. I am just sick with disappointment . . . his betrayal has shamed all of us.

I remember when Papa, Clara, and I read *A Christmas Carol*, about Mr. Scrooge, the rich man with no friends. We loved the story because Scrooge ended up a changed man with a generous heart. I know anything is possible with God, but I don't know if Jesse Blue cares.

## MONDAY, THE 4TH OF JUNE

Wash day. There is more work now, but we don't mind, we're so happy to have Papa home. We also wash clothes for Sam and Captain Clinkingbeard.

News from back East finally reached us here at Miner's Creek: We have a new president of the United States, Zachary Taylor. He was sworn into office three months ago, March 4. This came to us by way of a newspaper printed at Sutter's Fort. Several issues of *Placer Times* were sold at our grocery store for one dollar, that's how we got a copy. Also bought fresh carrots and tomatoes.

At supper I read one of the stories out loud to everyone, but it is a dreadful story.

It seems that a few weeks ago dozens of Yankees made a rule that foreigners are forbidden at Sand Creek Bar, which is not too far from here. They also ran off the Mexican, Peruvian, and Chinese men who were working around Sutter's Mill and Sutter's Fort, told them to go back to their own countries. When some of them put up a fight, vigilantes found a tree and hanged five of them! Then they jumped their claims and stole their gold. Vigilantes are men who take the law into their own hands. Sometimes they are honorable, but often they're just thugs who want everything to go their way.

Clara and I worry about Rosita and her family, but don't know how to protect them from vigilantes. At least Papa is home now and can help with the birth of her baby.

A wagon arrived this morning full of cats! They are strays that a ship captain collected in San Francisco. He is visiting mining camps, selling them for ten dollars each to help with rats that live in the garbage heaps. Papa bought us a kitten, a little gray thing with white paws. We named him Sergeant Boots.

This reminds me . . . before sundown I walked along the river to stretch my legs. It seemed that someone was following me, but every time I turned around nobody was there. Then a noise in the brush startled me. I saw what looked like a deer, but quickly realized it was too low to the ground and too swift, for as quickly as it appeared it ran off.

When I told Papa, he and the Captain returned with me to the spot. They studied the dirt for prints, following tracks up the hillside. Papa's face was pale when he announced that it was a mountain lion. He said from now on Clara and I must never walk alone. We must always keep careful watch of our surroundings for this big cat had been stalking me, he said.

## WEDNESDAY, THE 6TH OF JUNE

Well, first it was cats, today it was a bull with horns. It came into camp tied to the back of a wagon and is now corralled by itself, away from the other animals.

Clara and I didn't now why such a creature would be brought to Miner's Creek until we saw posters in town.

## Bull and Bear Fight, Come One, Come All No Bets Refused

We asked the storekeeper. He said it's a big event, only they have to catch a bear first. That's what some of the boys are doing now, out hunting a grizzly to bring back alive.

As we walked home we passed a blacksmith. He was hammering iron into a large cage on wheels. Several men with nothing to do stood watching, their thumbs hooked in their suspenders. They were making bets about the bear, whether or not it would fit inside the cage.

When we arrived back at the cabin Papa was out front, sitting by the stream with one of his friends. After introductions the friend explained he has quit panning for dust and now drives a mail wagon between mining camps and San Francisco. He charges four dollars a letter! If the letter then goes onto a ship for other parts of the United States, there are more costs. A thousand dollars a day is what he makes.

The man continued, "There's more money to be made off the miners themselves than by turning the earth inside out. Lord, that's hard work."

I glanced at Clara, but for once I kept my mouth shut. One thousand dollars was a fortune.

At supper I ladled fresh tomato soup into our bowls while Clara sliced johnnycake. Sam sat in the chair, as it is more comfortable for him than a stool. As soon as the Captain prayed over our food, my sister cleared her throat. She told Papa we thought he should hang out his shingle because the town needs a good doctor.

She and I had rehearsed a speech to convince him, so when he nodded, we didn't know what to say. He wiped his mouth with his napkin.

"Daughters, I miss helping people. I don't care if we're poor, my God, I miss it."

## BEFORE BED

With our money Clara and I purchased a hipbath from Dell's Fancy Store. It looks more like a feeding trough, but this evening we each took a long hot soak, behind our curtain. It was wonderful.

Papa bought a barrel of flour for forty dollars, but when Clara and I removed the lid we almost fainted. It was full of worms and stank like an outhouse! We rolled the barrel to the river, then dumped it, hoping the fish would eat the worms.

He also bought a pound of butter for six dollars and half a pound of cheese for three dollars. Captain Clinkingbeard paid sixteen dollars for a tin of sardines, two dollars for a tin of tea. Groceries are so expensive, it's no wonder most miners are poor.

Yesterday a grizzly mauled two men while they slept in their tent. Papa was called to help, but it was too late for one of them. The other lost his right ear and right eye and most of his scalp. Papa was able to stitch up his cheek where the bear had clawed him. When Clara and I saw the dead man being carried into town, we couldn't help staring. His face was completely gone and one shoulder had been eaten.

Then as we were walking back to the cabin, we caught a glimpse of the mountain lion in a distant tree. Actually, all we saw was its yellow tail hanging over a branch — the rest of it was hidden. Papa said these giant cats like high places so they can watch their prey. One pounce can kill a girl my size.

My sister and I can't decide what we're most afraid of: wild animals or a murderer who hasn't been caught.

## Tuesday, the 12th of June

We have another pet.

This morning I dipped a cup into our pail that Clara had just filled from the river. When I drank I felt something bump my upper lip. I held the cup up to the light and saw in the water a tiny speckled trout. So Clara washed out one of the bottles from our garden, a clear one, and filled it up in the stream. We made a funnel with a piece of paper to pour the fish down through the neck of the bottle. It is now swimming around in its new home in the center of our table. Sergeant Boots is also on the table, watching the fish closely. I wonder if this is how that mountain lion was watching me.

On the subject of pets, our burro sleeps outside now that Papa has returned home. We made a lean-to in the space between our cabin and the tent. With fresh hay on the ground it is quite cozy for her.

During the day we put Lilly in the corral with the mules and donkeys so she won't feel lonesome. She wears her hat only when we take her someplace, because the other animals try to nibble it.

## SATURDAY, THE 16TH OF JUNE

Today is Papa's birthday. Clara and I made a cake in our shovel, by setting a miner's pan over it like a lid. Since it was three layers it took three baking times, most of the day, in our outdoor fire. Truth be told, I burned the first two attempts because I took a walk and forgot we were cooking. Anyway, icing was powdered sugar and chopped walnuts.

Rosita and Tomás came for supper and to spend the evening with us. We all fancied up . . . Clara and I wore fresh aprons. Papa, Sam, and the Captain wore clean red shirts with blue suspenders. They looked like members of a fire brigade. We put fresh daisies in Lilly's hat and dressed Sergeant Boots in a little vest that we made out of an old sock. He didn't much like it; he kept trying to push it off with his front paw.

It appears that Rosita's baby will be born sooner than later, for she is quite round in the middle. She is relieved that our father is nearby.

Papa has some new patients. One is the dance-hall lady, but he won't say what the matter is. The others are three fellows up Waterfall Creek. They fell ill from eating mushrooms so Papa tended them until they were back in their right minds. He was paid with a plump hen, which he gave to Clara. She flung it over a tree stump and swiftly chopped off its head with her hatchet. After we plucked it, we roasted it on a spit outside, with plenty of salt and pepper. Cooking indoors makes the cabin too hot.

Back to Papa. Good color has returned to his cheeks and he is looking more robust. Yesterday the storekeeper asked him about Jesse Blue. Papa just shook his head and walked out of the store. Clara and I haven't brought up his name, we all get too upset.

## WEDNESDAY, THE 20TH OF JUNE

A grizzly was brought into town, hanging upside down from a pole between its legs, its paws tied together and its jaw muzzled. That's how the men carried it down from the hills. After they shoved it into the cage, someone cut the ropes so it could stand. Its claws were long and curved like daggers. When I saw it tossing its head with an angry noise in its throat, I felt sad. Even if this is the bear that bothered us or mauled those miners, I wish they would let it go free. I wish they wouldn't force it to fight a bull.

The men with nothing to do are now out beyond camp, building an arena. I saw it. It's a large circle of dirt, about forty feet across, with a rail fence surrounding it. An iron stake in the center is where the bear will be chained on the day of the fight. One of the men told me the bear will then attack from a sitting position and try to drag the bull down to the ground. But if the bull is stronger it will hook its horns into the bear. Either way, one of them will be killed.

Distressed by this news, I rushed back to the cabin.

## Friday, the 22nd of June

Bought groceries today. Bacon is fifty cents a pound, fresh eggs are still ten dollars a dozen, and a pound of brown sugar is sixty-two cents. The man with the chickens now has a milk cow so he makes butter and cream to sell.

There was another killing last night. This time, upstairs in the Blue Sky Hotel. The dance-hall lady found the body and ran out screaming; we could hear her from across the river. This fellow was shot. He bled all over the stairs.

Clara and I worry about a murderer still being on the loose.

I forgot to mention the man who cut his foot on broken glass. Papa gave him twelve stitches and is trying to keep him from walking in the dirt. If the wound gets infected, it could turn into gangrene. The man paid Papa with three ounces of gold dust, equal to forty-eight dollars.


## SUNDAY, THE 24TH OF JUNE

We wake every morning to the rooster crowing. We can hear him even above the noise of the rushing river.

Miner's Creek is suddenly deserted, except for most of the shopkeepers. Men have swarmed up to the North Fork of the American River because of a bonanza, that is, a strike, where two huge nuggets were found yesterday. One weighed forty ounces; the other was a bit over *twenty-five pounds*! Clara and I did the arithmetic. At sixteen dollars an ounce the small nugget is worth six hundred forty dollars; the big one nearly seven thousand dollars.

I don't know why one man has a lucky strike but others work hard to find only small bits of dust. Or why Papa wasn't the one to carve his name on that wall instead of Clara and me. He would have known to stake a claim, we did not. I don't understand why some things happen the way they do, such as why Mother was taken from us, but thieves and vigilantes run free. When I get to heaven, I'm going to ask God about all this. It makes my head hurt trying to figure out everything.

## LATER

I found a place to hide our money.

Clara and I dug a hole outside in the dirt under Lilly's bed. If anyone were to see us go into her little house, it will appear that we are just saying good night to our pet. During the day when she's in the corral, we rake her bed with clean straw and check to make sure our tin is still buried. It's been nearly a month, and no one has bothered us.

To keep any prowlers from reading this diary, I've hidden it in my satchel, wrapped inside my traveling dress. It's a bother to take it out when I want to write, but I feel more secure.

The days are hot, so we keep the door open. Flies and mosquitoes are a constant irritation, but no different than in Missoura. I'm surprised that I enjoy this heat! Papa explained that California is a drier climate than back home, and being high in the mountains makes the air feel lighter.

Sam is doing better, though his stump pains him greatly. His leg being amputated stopped the infection. Captain Clinkingbeard made him a nice crutch from oak. The handle is polished and smooth so it won't cut into Sam's arm when he leans on it. As soon as he is able to hobble around better, he will find his own place to live. He is a quiet boy, very polite, but I don't feel I can be myself when we're all under the same roof. Sometimes I feel like crying for no particular reason or because I am missing Mother. Sam always looks over at me as if he wants to help, but I do not need help.

Clara is the only one who understands about being a girl. When we get to feeling this way or that, we say, "Excuse us," to Sam as we pull our curtain closed. Then we whisper together or pray or cry in privacy. It seems we miss Mother more, not less. Some days thinking of her makes us smile, other days bring tears. I don't know why.

Finally I figured how we can make a window without buying one. With our hatchets Clara and I chopped a rectangular hole in our eastern wall, about eye level. Into this hole we've placed two dozen colored bottles from our garden, the necks facing outside. We filled the gaps with mud to keep the bottles in place. As we ate breakfast this morning such beautiful light was coming into the room, it reminded me of the stained-glass window in Mother's parlor in Missoura. This memory brings us joy.

## MONDAY, THE 25TH OF JUNE

The bull and bear fight will be next Sunday afternoon at two o'clock; cost is three dollars a person. I am curious to see what will happen, but Papa forbids us to watch.

I keep forgetting to write that Miner's Creek grows week by week with more stores and saloons, more miners. Some families with women and small children are up in the hills, but we've not met them yet. There's a gypsy woman in town who set up her tent on the main street. A big sign says PALM READER. Miners flock there because for ten dollars she tells fortunes. They all ask the same thing: *Where will I find the big strike?* Word is that she makes more money than her customers do.

Yesterday we saw a group of Tar Heads fresh from jumping their ship. One of them told Papa that San Francisco Bay now has two hundred abandoned vessels. Goods from all over the world are rotting in the hulls of these ships or are being looted. Some captains have had to put their crews in chains to keep them from leaving.

Papa said that gold fever is turning reasonable men into fools.

## SUNDAY, THE 1ST OF JULY

Clara and I discovered a crate of empty bottles behind one of the saloons. We weren't supposed to be walking there, but another gunfight had broken out on the street and we had to run for safety. We took the bottles home and with our axe cut off their lower halves. Then we stuck candles in the dirt by our cabin, lit them, and placed a bottle over each. The colored glass makes such festive light and the necks act as chimneys. We snuff out these lanterns before going to bed.

Sergeant Boots sleeps between Clara and me, on top of our blanket. He purrs quite a lot. I think he's happy with us, but his mouse-hunting job is not going well. Clara said it's my fault because I keep feeding him fish heads.

On the subject of fish, tonight I boiled a large trout in our kettle, one we caught with Mother's butterfly net. When it was cooked enough that meat was sliding nicely off the bones, I noticed something sparkly in the bottom of the pot. Captain Clinking-beard was sitting next to me in front of the fire. He leaned over to look, then smiled. It was gold, he said, sure enough.

Papa showed us how to brush the flakes into a cup where they can dry, then we'll have them weighed. It looks to be about half a teaspoon, maybe eight dollars' worth. From now on we will cook our fish in a pot instead of roasting them on sticks over the fire.

This "bonanza" reminded Captain Clinkingbeard of a story. Before we arrived in Miner's Creek, there was a funeral for a man killed in a gunfight. As his friends were lowering his casket into the hole, they noticed some glitter in the dirt. Immediately the coffin was pulled back up, set aside, and the friends started digging feverishly. After some days the hole had branched off into trenches, and the men were finding nuggets and flakes worth thousands of dollars.

At last they remembered their poor dear friend, but only because the body had begun to stink. So they laid him out under a pine tree and covered him with rocks.

Captain Clinkingbeard said he knows that story is true because he was one of those men. He felt so bad about disgracing his mate his gold fever cooled off. He just hardly cared anymore, about getting rich that is.

After hearing the Captain's tale, I understand why he and Papa get along so well. They just want enough to put bread on their table and sleep under a dry roof. At supper tonight when Papa prayed, he thanked God for providing the fish with gold in its belly.

"Lord," he said, "please grant us enough money so

we won't have to steal to eat, but not so much that we'll forget You. Thank you, amen."

## MONDAY, THE 2ND OF JULY

Days are blazing hot. Mosquitoes swarm around our faces every time we step out of the cabin. Near the river they swarm over every inch of us. There is nothing to do but spit them out of our mouths and stand in the smoke of our fire. Winter is the only cure for bugs.

The bull and bear fight for yesterday was postponed due to rain and thunder. The fight will be today in about an hour, so we are leaving town. Papa and Captain Clinkingbeard will be hiking around to check on patients. One miner needs some teeth pulled; another is suffering from chest pains. They live up Foxtail Creek.

Sam will stay here at the cabin. He's up and about now, but will never be able to get out into the hills unless it's on the back of a mule. His ribs have healed enough that Papa said he could take off Clara's corset. We washed it, dried it in the sun, then packed it away in Mother's trunk.

Just the other day I noticed Sam's eyes are beau-

## NEAR MIDNIGHT, I THINK

I am never going to have a baby! Rosita twists in pain every few minutes. Her face is red and she cries out in Spanish. I don't know what she's saying, but I know she's not happy.

## LATER

Just took a walk. The air is cool. I stood for a few minutes listening to the river and staring up at the canopy of stars. Across the valley is the dark shape of a mountain, outlined on both sides by speckled sky. It is a beautiful night. But I hurried back to the blazing campfire in case that mountain lion is nearby.

Clara is washing Rosita's face and neck, trying to make her comfortable. We are staying calm for her sake, even though we don't feel calm. I myself am terribly anxious. We've never done this before! I'm angry that Papa's not here, but it's not his fault he's so far away or that the baby decided to come early.

*Where is he?*

## Before dawn, maybe an hour

We have kept the lantern going all night. I am grumpy from no sleep. Rosita was so silent after her last pain that we became frantic, thinking she was dead. At last we realized she was in a deep sleep, that's all, because one minute later she was wide awake and breathless with another pain.

Clara and I have other worries that we keep to ourselves. Throughout these long hours we have heard rustlings in the woods, as if something is watching us. Every so often I carry the lantern outside, hoping its small flame will protect me from animals as I watch the trail for Papa. Just a prick of light in the distance could mean a torch coming our way. But it is dark.

## Morning

I am writing this in between sips of strong hot coffee. The campfire smells wonderful from the sausage and hotcakes some of Rosita's brothers are cooking, and the billowy smoke has chased away the mosquitoes.

One of the men just took out his pocket watch, clicked it open, then showed me it is 9:20.

Poor Rosita! She has been laboring for eighteen hours, her voice is hoarse. How I wish her mother or mine were here — even one of the new women from camp could help us, but they are too far away.

Oh — Clara's calling. . . .

## NOON

Finally, a moment to rest and write a few words . . .

After Clara called for me, I set my coffee in the dirt and hurried into the tent. She was at that moment lifting a tiny wet baby into her arms.

"It's a girl," she cried. There were tears in her eyes as she wrapped the little thing in a clean apron, then lay her in the crook of Rosita's arm. She has dark black hair, lots of it, and a wrinkled, scowling face. To me, she looked like a gargoyle, but I didn't say so. I'm learning not to speak my every thought.

# At the Cabin

By the time Papa arrived, we had cleaned up the bedding, washed the baby in a tub of warm water, and helped Rosita bathe, too.

Papa was astonished that everything went so well and said he might have to hire us as his assistants.

After examining mother and child, he declared both healthy and said Clara may stay with Rosita a few days to help. Papa and I will return then to see how they are and to escort my sister back home.

Tonight Sam and Captain Clinkingbeard are fixing supper, a chicken stew with dumplings. I see a ginger cake cooling on the shelf. Sam is whipping up some cream in a bowl to dribble over the cake. He gets around on his crutch quite well; in fact our dirt floor is dotted with "crutch prints." Sam now bunks with the Captain in his tent.

Before I forget, the baby's name is Esperanza. It means "hope."

There was another grizzly attack up Landlubber Creek. No one was killed, but it carried off a poor howling dog. I should have known the caged bear has a friend or two.

# WEDNESDAY, THE 4TH OF JULY

Late, about ten o'clock. I'm on my bed, the curtain closed around me. My candle sits on a little shelf Papa built into the wall above my pillow. It's as if I'm in my own cozy room because Clara is still with Rosita, our first time away from each other. I miss her! I wish I could whisper my secret to her, but for now will write it down. About today . . .

Papa loves the Fourth of July because his grandfather was one of the men who signed the Declaration of Independence. It's an important holiday to our family, so everyone took baths. Papa, Sam, and Captain Clinkingbeard went downstream to clean up. Where the river turns out of sight, there's a waterfall that pours into a pool deep enough for swimming. It is a pretty place, surrounded by boulders and baby pine trees. If my sister and I could be sure of privacy, we would go there daily. But since miners are working nearly every inch of the river, I bathed in the cabin.

After breakfast and chores we all went to town, even Sam on his crutch. The Captain carried a burlap sack over his shoulder with our picnic inside. The day was hot; a thermometer at Dell's Fancy

Store read 93 degrees in the shade. I wore the bonnet Clara made for me, to keep the sun off my face.

Papa wanted to listen to the men giving patriotic speeches. They took turns standing on a platform, built just this morning under the shade of a tall oak tree. Many were long-winded fellows who waved their arms and shouted. Some were miners complaining that foreigners take all the gold.

Finally about two o'clock in the afternoon an elderly white-haired man climbed the steps to the stage. He had fought in our war against England and he described the battlefields and bravery of General George Washington. He became choked up with the memories. When he read the Declaration of Independence, the audience was silent with respect.

After the old gentleman stepped down, the parade began. A band marched in front, which was really just three boys: One played a trumpet, another a fife, and one beat a drum. Then came a wagon with some miners sitting in back, proudly holding up their bags of gold. Six mules pulled the iron cage on wheels with the poor grizzly inside. His fur stuck out between the bars, he was squeezed in so tight. Following the bear came an assortment of men with no particular purpose, dressed in their best shirts and suspenders. It seemed they just wanted to be in the parade.

At last the crowd wandered through the streets, then out to the arena. The aroma of roasting meat came on the breeze. Papa asked what was cooking in the large fire pit.

A man standing next to us said it was the bull that was killed Sunday. The bear will be taken to Gouge Eye mining camp to fight another bull.

Must light a new candle . . .

Back to the picnic. My tenderhearted father did not want us to be around men guzzling whiskey or eating the spoils of a bear fight. So he led us to a meadow where a creek twisted its way among stones and wildflowers. It sparkled in the sunlight and looked so refreshing I quickly took off my shoes and stockings. The ice-cold water felt so good, and the little pebbles under my feet were soft as sand. Had I been alone with Clara I think we might have dunked ourselves, dresses and all.

Meanwhile Captain Clinkingbeard spread the burlap sack onto the grass, then laid out our dinner. Early this morning I had baked biscuits and stuffed them with crispy fried ham, tomato, lettuce, and red onion. We each had a plump juicy orange and a square of chocolate. I washed my sticky hands in the creek and had a drink at the same time. After eating, Papa and the Captain stretched out in the shade of a pine tree to nap. Sam and I were alone. We put our feet in the water (my two, his one) and talked through the afternoon. His eyes welled up when he spoke of his mother at their new home in Oregon.

"She is one of the kindest women on earth," he said. "Like you, Susanna. You are very kind."

I gulped in surprise. As I tried to think of what to say, Sam reached under my chin to untie my bonnet. He let it fall to the grass. I looked at him. His green eyes were gentle, and a breeze was lifting his hair off his shoulders. It struck me that Sam is handsome. He is not a boy at all. Something in me stirred, I don't know what it was, but suddenly I felt so hot I leaned forward to splash water on my face.

"I'm sorry, Susanna, I shouldn't have done that. . . . It's just that your face is so pretty, I wanted to see you better."

This is why I wish Clara were here, she could help me understand.

## MONDAY, THE 9TH OF JULY

Today I am fifteen years old. The rooster crowed right on time, but I didn't want to get out of bed, remembering with sorrow that Mother wasn't here to wake me as she always had done. But Clara was up early, cooking breakfast for me. Sunshine was glowing through our colored-glass window and a bouquet of fresh daisies was on the table.

"You're not lifting a finger today," she told me. "I'll do everything, all the chores, everything. Happy birthday!"

Papa presented me with a stool he had secretly made in the cabin of one of his patients. He had painted it a cheerful blue with yellow trim, and it is perfect for sitting outside. This is where I am now, writing with my journal on my lap. I was surprised to receive a gift from Captain Clinkingbeard: a piece of ivory, as white and flat as this page and on it, etched in black ink, is a beautiful drawing. It shows a clipper ship in full sail with a man in the bow and two young girls standing next to him. He called this art "scrimshaw" and said it is how he and other sailors passed their time on long sea voyages.

Clara is kneeling by the stream washing our supper dishes. Sam is sitting by the fire talking to Papa. Since our picnic a few days ago I feel shy when he smiles at me.

## LATER, ABOUT 10:00 P.M.

Everyone has turned in for the night so the cabin is quiet. Sergeant Boots is purring in my lap. To continue about today . . .

Clara baked brownies — she knows how I love them — so after supper the five of us sat around our table with a pot of tea. I am missing Mother, but otherwise this was the happiest birthday ever. Sam's gift to me . . . was the best. It all started this morning at sunrise. After breakfast I dressed Lilly in her hat and harness, which Sam loaded with some of his gear. We then walked upriver. He is nearly a foot taller than I am, but he bends over to lean on his crutch. It slows him down a bit, but he moves right along. I often forget he is missing a leg. With the sleeves of his shirt rolled above his elbows I can see that his arms are strong.

When the river branched off to a creek with a wide sandbar, we stopped. Sam pointed with his crutch.

Before us was a claim, neatly marked by four stakes. It blended across the bar into a rocky hillside.

This was his place before the explosion, he told me. Some rough fellows jumped it while he was sick, but the Captain and his shotgun helped him reclaim it. Just this week he has found nearly two hundred dollars.

Sam untied Lilly's pack and pulled out two wide pans. He gave one to me and demonstrated how to dip it in the stream, then swirl gravel. It was cold standing in the water! My dress was soaked up to my knees, but the sunshine beating down on my back kept the rest of me warm. Ten feet away, Sam kneeled on his one knee to work his own pan.

"Susanna," he said after some minutes. "You can come here anytime. Whatever gold you find, it's yours. See?" He nodded toward a piece of paper nailed to a board. I walked over to read it.

## Notice!

I, THE UNDERSIGNED, CLAIM THIS
PIECE OF GROUND, 900 SQUARE FEET,
FOR MINING PURPOSES AND FOR THE
BENEFIT OF MISS SUSANNA FAIRCHILD.
NO TRESPASSERS ALLOWED.

## SIGNED, SAMUEL JAMES
### JUNE 27, 1849

When I saw my name, I looked at him with questions.

He said Captain Clinkingbeard told him about the mine Clara and I had found, but lost. "You were in a hurry on account of me. Your family saved my life."

I didn't know what to say. I was stunned by his generosity, but wondered why my name and not my sister's. As if reading my silence, he said, "I spoke to Clara and she wants nothing to do with a placer. Maybe you and I can help your father earn back what Jesse Blue stole."

Sam got up, balancing on his leg as water flowed around his boot. He hopped to the beach, then leaned down for his crutch. He came over to me.

"Susanna," he said, "please forgive me if I'm being forward . . . but I love it when you and I are together. . . ." At this, he looked away. His face was red.

I picked up my pan and scooped it along the bottom of the creek, keeping my head down so he wouldn't see my sudden tears. I was overcome with how good he made me feel and wanted to tell Sam that *I* liked being with *him,* but didn't know how. When at last I looked at him, he smiled. Then, as if nothing had happened, we went back to our pans and talked about regular things. We worked for a couple hours, until the sun was overhead.

Must close . . . Clara just asked me to blow out the candle.

## TUESDAY, THE 10TH OF JULY

The mail wagon arrived to the usual excitement. Men line up outside the post office, which is really just a cubicle in one of the hotel lobbies. They wait for hours until someone has sorted all the packages and letters.

Sam is the only one we know who's received mail — two notes he read aloud to us after supper. One was from his mother in Oregon City. She had not yet heard about his leg. The other was from his brother, Virgil, who was himself recovering from an injury: Some children playing with a gun accidentally shot off three fingers of his left hand. I think if this dear mother ever sees her sons again, she will faint.

## LATER

Clara and I saw the man who stole Papa's money pouch. We immediately looked away so he wouldn't notice us watching him. He was leading a mule across the river into town. Draped over its pack-saddle was a dead bear cub. The sight of this poor little animal made me sad. At supper Papa told us the man tried to sell the bear's fur, but no one in Miner's Creek would buy it.

Papa keeps his gun by the door, loaded. He said he will trust God to deal with this thief, but he must still be ready to protect us from him.

## WEDNESDAY, THE 11TH OF JULY

A most terrifying event . . . my hand is shaking as I try to write. It is midnight, Clara and I are alone.

It started when Papa was called away after supper to tend some men wounded in a gunfight. All day the heat had been unbearable. Clara and I wanted to sleep outside under the stars, where the air was cool, but we knew it wouldn't be safe. It was still sweltering inside the cabin, so we decided to leave the door open. We pushed the solid log table to the threshold so it would block anyone from walking in. It left enough space for a breeze, and if Papa returned he could call to us. It seemed a good idea at the time.

It was so hot we slept on top of our blanket in our thin cotton petticoats. I woke to Clara's foot nudging mine. My eyes flew open. There was something in the doorway on the table. I could see its silhouette against the pale moonlight.

Mountain lion.

It was the size of a large, thin dog. Its face was in shadow, but I knew it was looking at us. I could hear Clara breathing fast; my own heart raced with terror. We were trapped. There was no way to reach Papa's gun without moving toward the cat. Because of the heat we had not built a fire in the hearth, so there was no way to make a torch.

I know Mother would forgive us for what we did next. Two of her books were on the floor by my side. Quietly I reached down for them and slipped one to Clara, all the while watching the animal that was staring at us.

Without a word my wonderful sister understood the plan. In one, swift moment she launched her book, then I did the same. Clara hit the mountain lion squarely on its nose, mine struck its cheek as it turned away. When it leapt off the table out into the night, I thought it was the most beautiful horrible thing I'd ever seen.

Papa has not returned, but we've latched the door, of course. Finally I'm calm enough to blow out the candle. We shall lie in the heat, thankful for these four good walls our father built.

## THURSDAY, THE 19TH OF JULY

The palm reader studied tea leaves to help the vigilantes catch the killer of those men. She said he would be a foreigner who lives alone. Well, they found him after someone pointed him out. He's in the hoosegow, to be hanged at sunset.

This morning, when Clara and I were at the store, we saw men sawing a hole in the platform where the Fourth of July speeches had been given. The oak tree had a rope draped over one of its branches. As we walked by, we overheard someone say that the murderer was a "no-good Mexican."

We told Papa.

"Why, those men should be ashamed of themselves," he said. "Less than a year ago this whole territory of California belonged to Mexico."

## BEFORE BED

Clara and I didn't watch the hanging. Papa had asked us to stay at the cabin; he didn't want us to see such a gruesome sight.

So, at sunset we sat by the river, on our rock. We could hear a rumble of voices, then the crowd burst into cheers. Papa was asked to be there because he's the only doctor around. Someone had to declare the man dead or they'd have to "string him up" again.

When Papa came home, his face was white. Clara and I sat with him by the fire — she rubbed his shoulders and I unlaced his boots. We didn't know how to comfort him.

Some minutes later he sighed. "This fellow was just a lad of seventeen," Papa said. His English was rough, but he kept pleading for people to believe that he had nothing to do with any killing. The one witness who accused him couldn't be found for questioning, yet those thugs went ahead with the hanging.

We are feeling wretched about this.

## NEXT DAY

Morning. Just finished breakfast, the dishes are drying outside.

Miner's Creek is astir with unpleasant news. Someone confessed to the murders last night, apparently sorry that an innocent boy was hung.

I am writing this quickly because Papa said we may attend the trial, today at noon.

## LATER

So much has happened. Good and bad. First, the good . . .

When we were around the fire last night, Sam asked Papa for permission to court me! Papa was so surprised he took his pipe out of his mouth and said, "What?"

"When I'm around Susanna," he said, "I feel like a

whole man, not a cripple." Sam glanced over at me, then shyly looked down. I wanted to faint, his words were so beautiful. Most of all I admired his courage saying them to my father.

So . . . Papa is going to think about Sam's request. I wish Mother were here to explain certain things such as courting — what is it anyway? I will ask Clara to teach me about hair. Maybe if I wear mine up off my neck, instead of braided, I'll appear more ladylike. When we were in bed, I asked if she was upset with me or if she felt left out.

Not at all, she said. Then she whispered a secret of her own. I'll write of it later.

This morning, before putting on my dress, I tried on Clara's corset. She cinched the ribbons so tight I was miserable. One minute later it was back in Mother's trunk. What a nuisance those things are.

Meanwhile, this pencil has worn itself down to a stub . . . will walk to town for another.


## MONDAY, THE 23RD OF JULY

For several days I have put off writing the awful news.

The trial was held in front of the hotel, on the

platform. When I saw the prisoner brought out from the hoosegow, I couldn't believe it.

It was the dance-hall lady.

Her hands were tied in front of her. She wore a blue satin dress with red trim along the sleeves and hem. A vigilante named the three victims. When he asked the lady if she had killed them, she spoke in a voice that surprised me.

"Gentlemen," she began. "I am guilty of one death, not three. He was a thief, a man without integrity." Then she said that no one listened to her when she asked for help. She admitted she shouldn't have taken the law into her own hands, but did.

"My silence yesterday cost the life of that poor boy — for that I am deeply sorry." Her voice was cultured and reminded me of Mother's. How did she end up alone in a mining camp?

Suddenly the thick rope was put around her neck, like a brown collar that came up to her chin. She was calm but asked the hangman for one favor. "Please allow me some modesty," she said.

He nodded, then tied a smaller rope around her knees so her dress wouldn't fly up when she dropped. That's when Clara and I turned away. We walked back to the cabin.

Papa came home later and wanted no supper. The woman died instantly, he said. And the crowd was so quiet you could hear the creak of the rope as she swung.

## FRIDAY, THE 27TH OF JULY

During the day the heat is fierce, but by sundown it cools off. I love living in the mountains.

My favorite time is supper, when the five of us sit around the campfire. The smoke blows this way and that, it stings our eyes and makes us cough, but it is a refuge from mosquitoes and, we hope, wild animals. This is when Captain Clinkingbeard tells stories. Tonight I learned my father has tales of his own.

After the hanging we remembered that the dance-hall lady had been one of his patients.

Was she sick? we asked.

No, he said. He stitched up some cuts in her hands. Someone had stolen her money, then tried to stab her. When she held up her hands to stop the blows, the knife made deep wounds.

"I never dreamed she had anything to do with a fella being killed." Papa said she was very well mannered and wanted to talk. She told Papa that some months ago she had come to Miner's Creek with her husband, but he had gotten pneumonia from standing in the cold rivers. When he died she was forced to earn her own living. Didn't know what else to do except dance in the saloons. She was trying to save money for a voyage back east, where the rest of her family lived.

Now she lies in an unmarked grave outside town. No one knew her name or even her husband's name. He had been buried somewhere along the North Fork.

## SUNDAY, THE 5TH OF AUGUST

Our day of rest wasn't at all restful, but wonderfully busy. Tomás and Rosita brought baby Esperanza and five of Rosita's handsome brothers.

They were here to help Sam build his very own cabin, just downstream, where the beach opens up into a glade. Papa and the Captain cut logs last week, so the walls were up in no time. By afternoon the roof was slanting skyward and wedged around a stone chimney. Sam himself cut out two windows and filled them with glass he'd bought in town. All this he did by hopping around, sometimes without his crutch.

Clara and I made sure there would be a good dinner. We set a kettle over the fire, simmering with three plump chickens, potatoes and tomatoes, onions and turnips. As the meat cooked, we scooped out the bones so by supper the stew was easy to eat. Rosita brought the Dutch oven. First we baked cornbread, then a sugary white cake, then some biscuits to eat with fresh butter.

Now everyone has gone home; Clara and I are both in bed. Though the cabin is stifling, we are keeping the door closed. Just when I think my sister is asleep, she starts whispering again. "*Antonio . . . Antonio . . .*" She can't stop talking about Rosita's brother, Antonio. He is about twenty years old and quite a gentleman. I remember him from our voyage and from all our visits to the Peruvian camp.

Anyway, Antonio has learned English well enough so that he and Clara conversed today as if they are old friends. At sunset he took out his guitar, and along with his brothers, serenaded us with beautiful melodies, first in Spanish, then English. When he sang "Dear Lady with the Soft Blue Eyes," we all turned toward my sister, but she was too charmed to notice our stares.

So that is Clara's secret. Her three days helping Rosita must have been filled with starlight and music.

## FRIDAY, THE 10TH OF AUGUST

This morning Sergeant Boots was on the table watching our pet trout. He pushed the bottle with his paw until it wobbled enough to fall over. Before I could rescue the fish, it poured out with the water down to the floor in a muddy splash. With one quick leap our cat scooped the flopping fish into his mouth. So that is the end of *that* pet.

## TUESDAY, THE 14TH OF AUGUST

Yesterday after doing all the wash, Clara and I picked flowers from the meadow. We made a bouquet, tying the stems together with a yellow ribbon. We walked out beyond town, past the arena to the little hill with crosses and wooden markers. Fresh dirt showed where the dance-hall lady had been buried.

We kneeled in the grass and placed the flowers on the mound. I recited a psalm, then Clara said, "We're sorry there was no one here to love you."

This morning we went with Papa to the lady's hotel room. The owner was there putting cosmetics and petticoats into a trunk to be auctioned off. Clara noticed a satchel under the narrow bed and rushed to retrieve it. When we saw a parcel of letters tied with string, Papa reached in his pocket for his money pouch.

"Sir," he said to the man, "I'll give you two ounces for the lady's bag, thirty-eight dollars."

"Doc, you got yourself a deal."

"Back at our cabin we read the letters, carefully unfolding the thin tissue paper. I felt embarrassed, as if we were peeking through a keyhole into someone's private room. But Clara and I wanted only to find her relatives, to let them know where she was buried. Maybe it was because we would never be able to visit our own mother's grave that we couldn't bear the thought of this lady being lost to her family.

So that is how we learned her name, Jenny Winslow of Deer Isle, Maine. From the letters we learned that her brother and nephews were eagerly waiting for her to return . . . her sister gave birth to twin daughters at Christmas . . . her parents sold part of their farm to a neighbor. . . .

This evening after supper Clara and I will sit down to write them. The next mail wagon going to San Francisco should be here tomorrow.

Sam cut two pieces of wood for us and notched them together in the shape of a cross. Next Captain Clinkingbeard did scrimshaw with his black ink, a beautiful drawing of a lady looking out at the mountains. Along the top he carved her name and the date she died — July 20, 1849. Now if Jenny's loved ones visit Miner's Creek, they'll be able to find her.

## FRIDAY, THE 17TH OF AUGUST

This afternoon Sam and I were sitting in front of the cabin, peeling potatoes for Clara's soup. Papa walked into camp and set his black bag in the dirt. He had been on the other side of the river, doctoring a man who broke his arm in a fight. Sitting down on one of the tree stumps, Papa unrolled his tobacco pouch and filled his pipe. He struck a match against a stone, held the flame over the bowl, and puffed until it was lit.

He squinted at Sam through his smoke. "I've done a lot of thinking," he said. "You're a hard-working fellow, and I've observed that you are honorable. I trust you to protect Susanna's virtue."

"Why, yes, sir, of course. Absolutely."

And that is how Papa gave permission for us to court. It only took him twenty-eight days to think about it.

## LATER

Summer is nearing its end. I can feel coolness in the early mornings and there's a sharp, cold smell at night when the campfire dies down. I asked Papa if we're going to live in Miner's Creek through the winter or push on to Oregon as we had first planned.

"I'm not sure what we should do," he said. He is concerned that Miner's Creek is too rough a town for Clara and me. Also, winters in these mountains are harsh. Last month Papa wrote friends as well as Aunt Augusta and Uncle Charles in Oregon, just to say what happened to Mother and to tell them where we are. They will be distraught to hear about her death, yet also surprised that we're in California. We never told them about our voyage because we knew we'd arrive on the West Coast before our mail. What we didn't figure on was our detour for gold.

No one knows this but I wrote a letter to "Mr. and Mrs. Jesse Blue, c/o Oregon City." I asked him to return Papa's gold, and maybe his wife will make him do so. She was one of Mother's dearest friends, after all. There was so much else I wanted to say, everything I've written in these pages, but I kept it simple, then signed my name. I pray that his heart will change like Mr. Scrooge's did.

*What will we do if we see him again?*

## NEXT DAY

This morning started out pleasant enough until I forgot my manners.

After breakfast Clara and I dressed up Lilly in her flowered hat and tied a picnic sack to her harness. It was a beautiful day to visit Rosita and her baby. I brought the colorful shawl she had given me on the ship, because it is becoming cool along the river and in the shady groves. We are ever looking about us for mountain lions, knowing they are quiet and hide themselves well.

It was so good to see little Esperanza. She is six weeks old and has much dark hair, more than Papa has! We took turns holding and rocking her while Rosita busied herself around the campfire. Clara's eyes were dreamy as she kissed the tiny nose and fingers.

"Oh, I love babies," she said. "I want one of my own."

"Well," said I, "you must have a husband first, everyone knows *that*." It felt good to boss my sister for once, but when I saw her face I wanted to take back my words. Her lip trembled as she tried to keep from crying.

"That's a mean thing to say, Susanna." She called me sassy. Then, because I wanted to have the last word, I said she was a terrible cook.

Poor Rosita didn't know what to do with two quarreling sisters. She just sang to her baby until she fell asleep, then tried to make cheerful conversation in her broken English.

On the trail back to the cabin I apologized twice, but Clara was too mad to listen. She kept her head high and marched with long strides ahead of me. Her dress made a snapping sound, like a sail in the wind.

Now we are back at the cabin. I'm writing at the table in a small pool of candlelight. Clara is in bed, turned toward the wall. She hasn't spoken to me since this morning.

Antonio must have been working up at one of the creeks because we didn't see him all day.

## SUNDAY, THE 19TH OF AUGUST

I woke early this morning and began cooking breakfast before Clara was out of bed. I fried bacon and onions, then stirred them into a skillet of eggs. Made one dozen corn muffins from a muffin tin I found last week by the river. Boiled a pot of good, strong coffee. Sunlight cast colors on the floor from our glass window and when I opened the door the whole room turned bright. Clara stepped out from behind our curtain in her nightgown and mussed hair. She looked at me.

"I shouldn't have let the sun go down on my anger," she said. "That's what Mother always told us, remember?"

137

At the mention of our sweet mother we both burst into tears and fell into each other's arms. After some moments we noticed three men standing in the doorway: Papa, Captain Clinkingbeard, and Sam. They looked bewildered and ready to help us. But we didn't need help.

Clara and I are the only ones who understand girl things.


## LATER

The *Placer Times* reports that our former President James Polk died of cholera. That was two months ago, on June 15. Mrs. Polk is especially sad because no children were born to their marriage.


## WEDNESDAY, THE 22ND OF AUGUST

Spent the day with Sam up at his claim. Captain Clinkingbeard came as well. We sifted out nuggets and dust that weighed one pound, nine ounces on the Captain's little scale, nearly four hundred dollars worth. Sam split it three ways, even though they did most of the work. I just scooped up gravel.

In my heart I worry about Sam. It has been difficult for him to kneel in the cold water for hours on end. He told us that after a day in the river his leg aches so bad he lies awake at night. I worry because placer mining is the hardest work on earth, and it is wearing him down and out, like it did Papa.

Right now Clara and I are in bed. Papa is outside by the fire with Sam; they've been talking for at least two hours.

## Sunday, the 26th of August

In the middle of the night I woke suddenly and sat up in bed. I finally figured out that since Jenny Winslow killed one man and not three, a murderer is still on the loose.

Rosita and Tomás came for supper with Esperanza and Antonio. Our evening was not as jovial as our last Sunday together because Papa brought up the subject of Oregon. When asked why not just winter in San Francisco, he explained that we have family up north. Since he has taken Clara and me so far away from home, he wants us at least to be near relations. We have aunts, uncles, friends, and my favorite cousin, Hattie, who is the same age as I am.

My heart is heavy on two accounts. Clara and Antonio looked miserable during this conversation. If we leave Miner's Creek they probably will never see each other again, and I know this would upset my sister a great deal. My other heartache is because of Sam. We have grown quite fond of each other, and I would be distressed if we had to say farewell.

Antonio took out his guitar after supper. He sang only in Spanish this time. Clara and I went to bed without our usual late-night chatter. We weren't angry with each other, just sad.

We don't know what Papa will decide.

## NEXT DAY

I love to sit outside after chores. For some reason the stool Papa made is a comfort to me. Often I just listen to the river and watch animals. A flash of blue up in a tree means a blue jay has landed. Squirrels leap from branch to branch, chasing one another in circles down the trunk then back up again. They make me laugh. And there's our gray kitty with the white paws. Sergeant Boots is always on the lookout for birds and has caught several — I don't know what kind, but I often see little brown feathers lying scattered among the pine needles.

The sun is pleasantly warm, not too hot. It is lower in the sky now, so the trees along the river cast lacy shadows over our camp. I think autumn will come sooner than what we're used to.

Tonight Papa wants to talk with Clara and me about Oregon. He wants us to tell him what we think, but I think so many things! It's just that I don't know what is best.

## TUESDAY, THE 28TH OF AUGUST

Made hotcakes for breakfast, the dishes are washed and put away. Clara and Captain Clinkingbeard are walking to town for flour and coffee beans. At last I have a moment to sit at the table and write.

Last night we agreed with Papa that it is best for the three of us to continue on to Oregon, though there was a lump in my throat as we talked. It will be as we had planned. As Mother had dreamed. We sat in the cabin by the fireplace, where a low blaze warmed us against the evening chill. Papa smoked his pipe and looked around at our cozy furnishings.

When he asked Clara about Antonio, I expected her to dissolve into tears. But she didn't. She gazed into the fire and turned her palms upward, as if asking a question. After a moment she said, "I will miss him very much."

Papa then looked at me. I wish I could say I was as brave as my sister, but I struggled against tears. "Papa, I love Sam."

He drew on his pipe, nodding.

So that is how our evening ended, quietly.

## WEDNESDAY, THE 29TH OF AUGUST

Didn't sleep well last night.

We will be buying a wagon and mules this week for our journey. Lilly is still too little to bear any great load, so my favorite pet will have to stay behind in Miner's Creek.

I suppose I'm elated about finally settling in

Oregon and once again being with family. I will miss the mountains and the wild beauty of its rivers. I will miss the excitement of gold, at least the possibility that one of us might stumble upon the next big strike. I will miss Captain Clinkingbeard and his stories, as well as Rosita and her large family.

Last night when I was getting undressed for bed I heard Papa and Sam outside. I quickly leaned against the door with my ear pressed to a crack, straining to listen. Sam was talking about how he loves his new cabin and about his brother over in Mokelumne Hill, but that's all I really heard. I want him to come to Oregon with us! Can I tell him this? In a courtship is it proper for a girl to say such things or must everything be *his* idea?

I'm confused and upset. How I wish Mother were here.


## TUESDAY, THE 4TH OF SEPTEMBER

These past days have gone by quickly and much has happened, so I'll be brief.

When we awoke this morning the ground was dusted with snow. It was frosty outside, but by noon the snow had melted. Trees high up in the hills are turning golden and red, and their leaves are falling with the breeze.

Tomorrow we leave Miner's Creek (TOMORROW!).

Rosita and Tomás will live in our cabin with baby Esperanza because they are staying through the winter. Sergeant Boots will be their good cat, and they will watch over Lilly.

A shootout last night at the Mad Mule Saloon landed four men in the hoosegow and four full of bullet holes. Their bodies were displayed on Main Street, propped up inside their open coffins. Clara and I happened by, not realizing why the crowd was there until we saw for ourselves. It was gruesome, but I couldn't stop staring. Their faces were purple and bloated. Flies swarmed over the wounds. At sunset some men nailed the coffin lids shut, loaded them on wagons, then hauled them out to the cemetery. A trial will be held tomorrow. If there are to be any hangings, fortunately we will be gone.

Well, I haven't been as brief as I planned. Clara is calling for me to help with supper so I will finish later. . . .

Most everything is packed. We have two crates by the door full of food and cooking things. I hope I can sleep.

Earlier I didn't have time to write why I am so cheerful.

Sam is coming, too! He and Captain Clinkingbeard have their own little wagon and mule team, so they will take the trail with us to Sacramento. Sam's brother, Virgil, wrote that he won't be returning to Oregon yet. He will stay in Mokelumne Hill until next summer because his claim still brings him a few hundred dollars a week. Despite his missing fingers he wants to "work 'er till she's dry." That's what his last letter said.

I forgot to mention why the Captain is coming with us. When he learned of our plans to leave, he told us a story that brought Clara and me to tears. . . .

Three years ago he was sailing a schooner around the Sandwich Islands, with his wife and two young daughters aboard. When they anchored in a cove, friendly natives paddled out to the ship with fresh fruit and other gifts. They climbed aboard and were welcomed by the passengers and crew. After some minutes, however, Captain Clinkingbeard noticed the natives were feverish and had blisters on their chests and faces. By the time he recognized the signs of smallpox, it was too late. Everyone on deck had been exposed. Within days many of his Tar Heads and passengers were dying, including his beloved wife and daughters; the girls were just eight and twelve years of age. Because the Captain had been vaccinated as a child, he didn't fall ill.

Burying them at sea, he told us, broke his heart. He no longer loved the ocean. That's why abandoning his ship in San Francisco and heading for the hills was so easy to do.

At that Clara and I burst out, "Oh, do come with us, Captain, please. We want you to."

His eyes were moist. When he ran his hand over his beard, the bells made the tiniest bit of music.

## ON THE TRAIL

I am sitting in the back of our wagon; Papa and Clara are sharing the reins in front. It is rather bumpy to be writing, but I will try.

About a mile behind us are Sam and the Captain.

They are keeping that distance because of the dust our wheels stir up. Last night we camped outside Sutter's Fort. It looks much as it did when we passed through six months ago. All sorts of men are busy hurrying for gold country. I don't mention this to Papa, but I am always looking at faces, wondering if we'll see Jesse Blue. It's still hard to believe our old friend no longer cares for us.

As we were saying our good-byes to Rosita and Tomás, her brothers began building bunks into Sam's cabin. All seven of them will stay warm this winter in front of that little fireplace. I'm pleased knowing friends will enjoy our cozy log homes, and that our hipbath will get good use.

Antonio and Clara shook hands as a gentleman and a lady. He bent forward to kiss her cheek, but she turned away and climbed up into our wagon. Her back was to me so I couldn't tell if she was crying. She sat stiffly for some miles. Finally she looked over her shoulder at me and said, "Oh, Susanna, we're on our way!"

It has started raining. Papa just turned around from his seat to say he wants to keep going. Well, then, I shall pull a tarpaulin over my head and watch the scenery. More later.

*　　*　　*

Sacramento is a boomtown! While waiting for a boat to take us downriver, we walked around the wharves, or what they call the *embarcadero*.

When we were last here, lots were priced at five hundred dollars each. Now they are selling for five thousand dollars! "Ready Cut" houses are being hammered together throughout town, along with stores and a magnificent new hotel fit for Queen Victoria. Clara and I were delighted to see women in beautiful satin dresses walking here and there (most were wearing corsets, we were certain). Oh, the charms of a bustling city.

We are not rich, but we have enough gold to stay the night in a hotel and buy passage for the riverboat. We'll sell our wagons and mules, sail downstream to San Francisco, then wait for the next ship sailing north to Oregon.

By the way, it is warmer here than Miner's Creek. A large thermometer in front of a café reads 87 degrees. Once again it feels like summer.

## Aboard the *Lady Luck*

We're on the Sacramento River, heading west toward the sea. It is, of course, much faster than when we sailed up against the current. I am sitting on the floor of the deck, leaning against the soft fabric of my satchel. A breeze off the water makes it pleasant to be in the sun. My bonnet is packed away for now, and my hair is braided as usual. I lost interest in combing it up fancy like Clara's because my arms grew tired — it is such a chore. Perhaps in Oregon I will work harder at being a lady.

Sam is sitting in the bow with Papa and Captain Clinkingbeard. Clara is lying next to me, her head pillowed on her shawl. She's watching the clouds — I think she'll soon be dozing.

It is beautiful along this river. Wild grapevines hang from tree limbs over the water, making shady arbors as we drift by. Here and there our boat steers around little islands that are forested with oaks and manzanita. Smoke from a campfire rises above the trees, bringing a delicious aroma of roasted meat. Papa said Indians live here. A trail on the south bank is lined with sunflowers, like bright yellow faces saying hello. I will miss California.

At this moment we are passing an adobe ranch house. I can see a señora hanging up her wash and her dark-haired children playing. Now they are hidden by a curve in the river.

Oh, Papa is asking if we might have some dinner. It's noon, so I'll write later.

We ate boiled eggs, crackers, cheese, and crisp red apples we bought in Sacramento. We sat together on deck, I next to Sam, quietly enjoying this last bit of gold country. I am happy Captain Clinkingbeard is with us. Without saying so, we have become his family. Now *he* is like our uncle, a pleasant dear man who tells stories and listens to ours.

After the Captain said he would come to Oregon with us that day, I walked over to Sam. He was sitting by the river, cleaning some fish he had just caught. When I asked if he had decided about Oregon, he set his knife down and smiled up at me.

"Susanna," he said, "I can't wait to see the looks on my parents' faces when they meet you. Does that answer your question?"

I felt myself blush. Yes, I said. My voice was flat, but inside, my heart was leaping.

And here we are.

## SUNDAY, THE 9TH OF SEPTEMBER, SAN FRANCISCO

Our hotel is so noisy none of us slept last night. The walls are just thin strips of canvas hanging from the ceiling. Clara and I could hear two ladies arguing in the next room. And against the other wall we could see silhouettes of men taking off their shirts and trousers. We were so embarrassed we blew out our candle early and covered our heads with pillows.

Now we are dressed and waiting in the lobby for Papa to pay our bill — seven dollars for two filthy rooms. We are covered with fleabites all over our arms and legs and in places where it's not polite for ladies to scratch.

I wonder if the hotel next door is as dirty. I laughed when I first saw it because it is a *ship*. Somehow men were able to haul an abandoned vessel from the bay onto shore. They wedged it between two buildings, built a ramp leading up to its deck, and turned it into a rooming house. We saw others like it along the street facing the ocean. Captain Clinkingbeard noticed his own ship propped up on a wharf, now a loud saloon. We saw dancing ladies on deck. They leaned over the rail and called down to men passing in the street.

Papa is here; it's time to go. A carriage is waiting for us out front to take us to Pier Eight where our next voyage begins. I bought a newspaper to read later so I will tuck it into this journal.

## WAITING ON THE DECK

While men load our ship with supplies and luggage, Clara and I are sitting on a trunk. A nearby seagull is perched on a piling; he is watching Clara eat a biscuit. The cries of gulls fill the bay as they circle little fishing boats that come and go. I love the smell of the ocean.

## ABOARD THE *SANTA CATALINA*

We've just sailed through the Golden Gate and once again are at sea, this time aboard a three-masted schooner. There are approximately sixty passengers, mostly rough-looking men, but we did count five women and two children. Clara and I are relieved to have the clutter and babble of San Francisco behind us, and I think our beds tonight will give us good rest. We have a cozy cabin with a porthole facing east, which means we'll have a view of the coast the whole trip. Depending on weather it should take four or five days.

It is cold as winter! I'm wearing Rosita's colorful shawl and we are warming our room with an oil lamp. Clara is resting on her bunk. We have nearly an hour before supper so I'll try to get a few thoughts down.

Being at sea reminds me of Mother, but I am not in despair. Somehow our six months in Miner's Creek was a good place for me to reflect. There were just three of us, now there are five. Papa is ready to be the good doctor he'd wanted to be in the first place. We have enough gold to buy land and build the little house of Mother's dreams. I feel closer to her because of this.

Supper bell . . . must go!


## BEFORE BED

Clara and I are in our nightgowns. She is reading an adventure story called *The Three Musketeers*, so we are sharing lamplight. We are a bit queasy from the rolling of the ship, but not nearly as ill as on our first voyage. I haven't yet told her about this evening.

At sunset Sam and I strolled on deck under the full, white sails. The glowing sky made the water look pink, and there were dolphins leaping above the swells alongside the bow. The wind made our voices seem small, and the deck was wet from sea spray. This was how I slipped and fell against Sam. But before I could gather myself, he enfolded me in his arms and bent down to kiss me. For the rest of my life I will feel silly for what happened next: I burst out laughing. I don't know why.

Sam had the grace and good humor to laugh as well.

Surely he is now lying on his bunk, wondering what sort of girl he is courting. Clara just looked at me over the top of her book and asked why I am smiling.

I'll tell her after we blow out the light. I am glad I have a sister to talk to.

# NEXT DAY, AT SEA

The forests of Oregon Territory are now off our starboard side as we sail north. It is so green and pretty. I wish the captain of this ship would anchor and let us row to shore, but he says the best place to stop will be up the Columbia River in a harbor called Fort Vancouver. From there it'll take another day or two by wagon to reach our new home.

The breeze is cold, but the fresh salt smell is wonderful. There are places to sit out of the wind, such as among water barrels and the thick coils of rope. Most of the passengers stay below where it is warmer. This morning a longboat that is usually stored upside down on deck was rolled upright so that it could air out. Clara and I climbed inside and settled low between the benches, wrapped in our shawls. We were as snug as if in a little sunroom. It was here that I remembered the newspaper.

I took it from between these pages and unfolded it carefully so the breeze wouldn't take it. It's just one sheet, printed on brown paper. My eyes fell on a story that I immediately read aloud to Clara.

Sometime last week a fire destroyed one of San Francisco's rooming houses, burning nearby buildings before the flames were put out. Fortunately no one was killed. The article reported that one of the miners who fled for his life was now suing the landlord. It seems that this fellow had kept a safe in his room to protect his money. But when he returned to the ruins the following day and combed through the ashes, he found only a chunk of melted iron. His cash — some four thousand dollars — had turned to cinder. The man filing the lawsuit? Jesse Blue of Oregon City.

My sister and I gathered our skirts to climb out of the longboat. We found Papa belowdecks, playing cards with the others. After I read the story, he looked sad.

"I'm sorry for Jesse," he said, shaking his head. "He chose money over friendship, but now he has neither."

## LATER

Back in the longboat . . . it's nearly noon judging by the short shadows on deck. The navigator is glancing at the sun to take measurements from his sextant. Next to him stands our captain, scanning the horizon with his spyglass. Overhead, high in the masts, sailors are flung over the yardarms to adjust sails, their feet balanced on a thin walking rope. I feel nervous watching. If one of them falls, there is nothing to catch him. They're all working hard, but I wonder, were they put in chains so they wouldn't jump ship in San Francisco?

I also wonder about gold fever, why it makes some men crazy and others wise. Such as Sam, my father, and Captain Clinkingbeard. They suffered heartbreak and loss, just as Jesse Blue had, but they didn't become thieves or liars. *Why?* I asked Papa. *What makes the difference?*

His eyes were gentle when he looked at me. "Susanna, it seems that true character often isn't revealed until a person is faced with temptation."

And so, as I gaze out at the rolling sea, I ponder my father's words.

## FORT VANCOUVER

I am writing from a small log cabin inside the walls of this fort, where Clara and I have been welcomed by one of the soldier's wives. We will be here another day or two until Papa can arrange for a wagon and horses. Meanwhile he, Captain Clinkingbeard, and Sam are camped outside the walls, along a stream that flows into the great Columbia River. Mountain men and fur traders are camped there as well, many living out of tepees. I have seen my first Indian, a woman with long black hair, carrying a baby on her back.

It is hard to believe we are nearly home. I think I will love Oregon Territory for it is beautiful. Lush pine forests come right down to the sea and are thick along the rivers and streams.

I am to the end of Mother's diary. It seems she has been with me on this long journey after all, through these pages and my thoughts. I miss her, Clara and Papa miss her, but we will start our new life with her dream.

There's a small window looking out to the fort's busy courtyard. I can see Sam! He is walking this way, leaning on his crutch. My heart feels light at the sight of his clean shirt and freshly barbered face. He is carrying a bouquet of wild fern tied with a white ribbon. I will close Mother's journal now.

Sam has come a'courting.

# EPILOGUE

When the Fairchilds arrived in Oregon City, their relatives and friends were overjoyed to see them. Three weeks later a new wave of emigrants also arrived, after six grueling months along the Oregon Trail, many of them from Missouri. Among them was one of Susanna's childhood friends, Betsy, now a bride with an infant son.

Until he was able to build his own house, Papa and the girls stayed with Aunt Augusta, Uncle Charles, and their young cousins, Bennie and Jake. Over the years Dr. Fairchild's medical practice flourished due to his skill and his kindness.

The day after Sam put glass windows in his new cottage he and Susanna were married in a field of wildflowers, surrounded by their families and friends. They had five daughters in five years, then a set of triplet boys who died at birth. Susanna lived out her days next door to her cousin Hattie and across the road from their friend Betsy.

Sam's twin brother, Virgil, returned to Oregon

with enough money to build a luxurious hotel, and they went into business together. Brothers Inn was host to three United States presidents and scores of other dignitaries.

Clara never married. Because of her love for children she started an orphanage and became known throughout the area as the adored "Aunt Clara." She lived to the age of 101.

Captain Clinkingbeard married a young widow from Missouri whose husband had drowned when crossing the Snake River. The Captain adopted her two children, then they had seven of their own. After his voyage from San Francisco he never returned to the sea. He earned his living as a wood-carver.

When Susanna and Clara visited Mrs. Blue, they learned she hadn't received Susanna's letter. She didn't know her husband had stolen Papa's money, so the girls decided to keep the matter to themselves. Jesse Blue was never heard from again.

# LIFE IN AMERICA
## IN 1849

# HISTORICAL NOTE

When President James Polk addressed Congress on December 5, 1848, he made statements that electrified Americans. He confirmed that there was indeed gold in their new territory of California, bought just a few months earlier from Mexico. In fact the mines were "more extensive and valuable than was anticipated." Four days later Horace Greeley's *New York Daily Tribune* proclaimed, "We are on the brink of the Age of Gold."

Yes, gold! The rumors were true after all. The rumors had persisted for many years, but here was confirmation from the President himself. The United States had just acquired the California territory ten months earlier in the Treaty of Guadalupe Hidalgo, which ended the war with Mexico. The United States paid fifteen million dollars in return for the territories of California, New Mexico, and the Rio Grande region.

Mexico had failed to act on the rumors of gold in California. It already had productive copper, silver, and gold mines in its districts of Guanajuato and

Sonora. Why bother with California, just a remote and sparsely populated province? This indifference made it easier for Mexico to sell California to the United States.

The timing couldn't have been better for America.

On January 24, 1848, nine days before the treaty was signed, there had been a momentous discovery in California. While working at Sutter's Sawmill on the American River, a man named James Marshall found gold in the tailrace, which is the part of a mill where the river flows after spilling over the waterwheel. Marshall, a former farmer and wheelmaker from New Jersey, shared the discovery with his partner, John Augustus Sutter, a gregarious and highly ambitious German-born Swiss merchant.

Sutter had wandered the New World, suffered more than one bankruptcy after fleeing creditors, and eventually found himself in California in 1839. He persuaded the Mexican governor of California to grant him fifty thousand acres of land, located east of San Francisco Bay, at the confluence of the Sacramento and American rivers. Here Sutter began anew his dreams of a business empire, building a fort. He called it New Helvetia, although everyone else called it Sutter's Fort. He also bestowed upon himself the title of captain, for supposed service in the Swiss Guard of Charles X of France. New Helvetia was eventually renamed Sacramento in 1848.

In 1847, Sutter took Marshall into a partnership. It was while Marshall and some workers were establishing the sawmill that the discovery was made. A worker's diary briefly noted: "Monday 24th this day some kind of mettle was found in the tail race that looks like goald first discovered by James Martial the Boss of the Mill."

Within weeks of Marshall's discovery of "goald," Captain Sutter complained that all his able-bodied employees had deserted his sawmill, his fort, ranches, and stores and had become miners themselves. By mid-May of 1848, the streets of San Francisco were empty, as nearly every citizen — some eight hundred people — had headed for the gold fields.

They were just a small advance party compared to the deluge of humanity to follow the next year. The vision of striking it rich captured the imagination of Americans — and foreigners — everywhere. Overnight people quit jobs, abandoned their farms and families, and sought the quickest way to California to find their fortune in the creeks, rivers, and the western slopes of the Sierra Nevada. They were eventually called the Forty-niners, for the year the stampede began. Because so many of these prospective miners came by sea from distant shores, another name for them was Argonauts, after the men in Greek mythology who sailed with Jason in search of the Golden Fleece. Natives and foreign-born residents of the Hawaiian Islands sought passage on every ship bound for San Francisco; South American miners sought ships bound for North America; Mexicans sailed from Mazatlán.

In May 1848, only a few hundred gold seekers were mining. By the end of the year there were between six thousand and ten thousand as the news traveled fast.

Ultimately hundreds of thousands of people participated in one of the largest voluntary migrations in history. They were not just miners, but also part of the huge supporting cast. Merchants, blacksmiths, saloon keepers, carpenters, washerwomen, and entertainers often made more money than the Forty-niners themselves. Though the actual rush lasted less than a decade, $465 million worth of gold was uncovered and dozens of mining towns sprouted up throughout California. It was on its way to becoming one of the most populous states in the Union.

*     *     *

There were several ways for Easterners to travel west. At the time overland routes took six months and cut through vast deserts, prairies that were inhabited by many Indian nations, and then over rugged mountain passes. Another route, which took between five and twelve months, was by sea, around Cape Horn, the southern tip of South America. This in itself was harrowing because of the unpredictability of the weather. If a ship floundered in violent storms, her crew and passengers might vanish without a trace. Unlike a wagon breaking down on the trail, there was no way for other travelers to help.

The quickest route was across the Isthmus of Panama, which took just weeks instead of months. This narrow neck of land was about seventy-five miles across, but it was a swampy jungle, infested with mosquitoes. Poor sanitary conditions often led to diseases such as malaria and cholera. Alligators, poisonous insects, and snakes added to the dangers. Unfortunately many fortune seekers died before ever reaching California.

This route was taken by the scores of Forty-niners who swarmed the docks of New Orleans after President Polk's speech. Within two months eight thousand

Americans had boarded vessels headed for Chagres, on the Caribbean side of the isthmus. From here they trekked west to Panama City, a shabby town that overlooked the Pacific Ocean. Here they waited. They knew that whalers and merchant ships would eventually arrive and could transport them north to San Francisco.

One such vessel was the *California,* a side-wheeler steamship on her way from New York to provide mail service along the Pacific Coast. Her journey around Cape Horn, actually through the Strait of Magellan, had been slowed because of storms. Captain Cleveland Forbes had no idea that fifteen hundred men were waiting for him in Panama City, for he had been far out to sea when the rest of the country learned the tantalizing news. One glitch in Captain Forbes's arrival was that he had anchored earlier in Callao, Peru, for supplies and allowed seventy Peruvians on board.

The sight of foreigners on a United States vessel bound for United States goldfields enraged the waiting Americans. These Peruvians were considered trespassers, thieves who would be taking what didn't belong to them. Sadly this was just the beginning of xenophobia, the hatred or fear of foreigners that would become rampant in coming years. By the end of 1849, some ninety thousand people had headed for California, and nearly twenty-three thousand were not U.S. citizens.

Gold fever also spread to the Oregon Territory, where much of its population had recently emigrated from the East. Without a glance backward hundreds of men left their work and families for a chance at a fortune. By October 1848, about three thousand Oregonians had arrived in California, some of the first Americans to reach the goldfields. This was two months before President Polk gave his unforgettable message to Congress.

Marshall and Sutter never profited from the California Gold Rush. Both died bitter and penniless. Marshall's mining claims were swept aside, and he eventually became a blacksmith in a little town near Coloma, site of the first discovery. His last years were spent in abject poverty. He died in 1885 and was buried on a hill overlooking the site where he had bent down thirty-seven years earlier for the discovery that changed the course of United States history.

Sutter's decline was more spectacular, as he was prone to grandiose plans and gestures. For a brief period he was one of the most important men in the American West and ran unsuccessfully for governor of California. Ultimately his lack of business savvy led to his downfall. Once again, his willingness to incur vast debt led to severe problems with his creditors. He was forced to sell Sutter's Fort. Later, he lost his last remaining property, a ranch, to a flood and suspected arson. He then moved to Washington, D.C., to persuade Congress to grant him $125,000 for what he claimed was owed him as reimbursement for aid furnished to California emigrants. After fifteen years, and seemingly on the brink of successfully realizing his claim in 1880, Sutter died in his sleep.

Note:

**The drowning of Mrs. Fairchild in *Seeds of Hope* is fiction. There is no record of a woman being swept overboard from the decks of the *California*, although the voyage around the Horn or through the Strait of Magellan was one of the most treacherous ordeals for the Argonauts. Dozens of ships did meet tragic ends during the Gold Rush, with all aboard perishing.

**The bull and bear fights that took place in early California provided jargon for Wall Street that is still used today. When the animals were brought into the ring, the bear was tethered to a chain. It would dig a hole several inches deep and lie down. From this hole it would fight, either in a prone or sitting position. The bull would stand. Thus, in America's financial centers a bull market means stocks are going up; a bear market means stocks are going down.

**Hoosegow* is slang for a guardhouse or jail. It comes from the Spanish word, *juzgado,* meaning court of justice.

When President James Polk confirmed that gold had been discovered in California, the newly acquired territory became a magnet for those seeking the riches gold would provide. From all over the country and all over the world, people found their way to California. Some traveled over land, but others who could afford it got there quicker by crossing the Isthmus of Panama, which cut the trip from the east to west coast down to weeks instead of months.

When ships arrived in San Francisco Bay, the possibilities were so enchanting that along with the passengers, the crew often abandoned the ship. The result was a "town" of ships on the bay. This ship, Euphemia, became San Francisco's first jail.

173

The year 1849 brought so many people to California that a guide was created to help the settlers find their way in this golden land. It helped them figure out the terrain and routes around the area, but most importantly, it instructed them how to find gold.

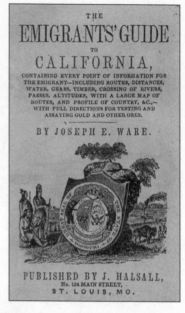

THE
# EMIGRANTS' GUIDE
TO
## CALIFORNIA,
CONTAINING EVERY POINT OF INFORMATION FOR THE EMIGRANT—INCLUDING ROUTES, DISTANCES, WATER, GRASS, TIMBER, CROSSING OF RIVERS, PASSES, ALTITUDES, WITH A LARGE MAP OF ROUTES, AND PROFILE OF COUNTRY, &C.,— WITH FULL DIRECTIONS FOR TESTING AND ASSAYING GOLD AND OTHER ORES.

BY JOSEPH E. WARE.

PUBLISHED BY J. HALSALL,
No. 124 MAIN STREET,
ST. LOUIS, MO.

Mostly, the miners were inexperienced. Indeed, some had dropped successful careers as doctors and lawyers to take a chance at striking it rich in the gold fields.

174

As women were few and far between in the region, the arrival of a single woman in a mining town was quite an event. The miners were so deprived of female companionship that they often proposed marriage at first sight.

Even though the corset was an important part of a young woman's life in the city, it was difficult to function in the rough conditions of the gold-mining communities while wearing these constricting and cumbersome pieces. Women's new lives in the wilderness gave them all the reason they needed to free themselves of this garment.

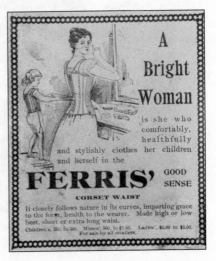

A Bright Woman

is she who comfortably, healthfully and stylishly clothes her children and herself in the

FERRIS' GOOD SENSE

CORSET WAIST

It closely follows nature in its curves, imparting grace to the form, health to the wearer. Made high or low bust, short or extra long waist.

Children's, 25c. to 50c.   Misses', 50c. to $1.00.   Ladies', $1.00 to $2.00.
For sale by all retailers.

Gold mining was a tough business. There were many methods employed by the miners, including filtering sand through a rocker that shakes out everything but the gold. However, after spending long days in the cold, mountain streams searching for gold, miners often came up empty-handed.

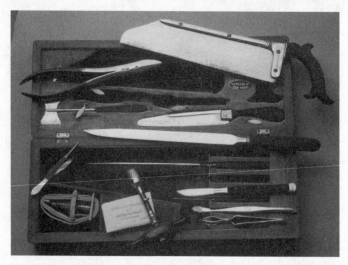

Aside from food, medical tools and medicines were the most vital, but least available supplies. This amputation kit was used to saw the limbs of the unfortunate miners who suffered accidents in the treacherous mining process.

# Miner's Griddle Cakes

Ingredients:

1 cup yellow cornmeal
1 cup all-purpose flour
1 teaspoon baking soda
1 teaspoon salt
1 teaspoon sugar
2 cups buttermilk
2 tablespoons vegetable oil
1 slightly beaten egg yolk
1 stiffly beaten egg white

1. Mix dry ingredients.
2. Blend in buttermilk, oil, and egg yolk.
3. Fold in egg white.
4. Let stand for ten minutes.
5. Spoon batter carefully onto hot griddle (frying pan) and cook.

Makes 16 four-inch pancakes.

*As ingredients and supplies were scarce, recipes were simple but hearty.*

# Clementine

*In a cavern, in a canyon,*

*Excavating for a mine,*

*Dwelt a miner, Forty-niner,*

*And his daughter, Clementine.*

CHORUS:

*Oh, my darlin', oh my darlin',*

*Oh my darlin' Clementine,*

*You were lost and gone forever,*

*Dreadful sorry, Clementine.*


*Light she was, and like a fairy,*

*And her shoes were number nine,*

*Herring boxes, without topses,*

*Sandals were for Clementine.*

CHORUS

*Drove the ducklings, to the water,*

*Every morning just at nine,*

*Hit her foot against a splinter,*

*Fell into the foaming brine.*

CHORUS

*Ruby lips above the water,*

*Blowing bubbles soft and fine,*

*Alas for me, I was no swimmer,*

*So I lost my Clementine.*

CHORUS

*A folk song about the Gold Rush, Clementine is still popular today.*

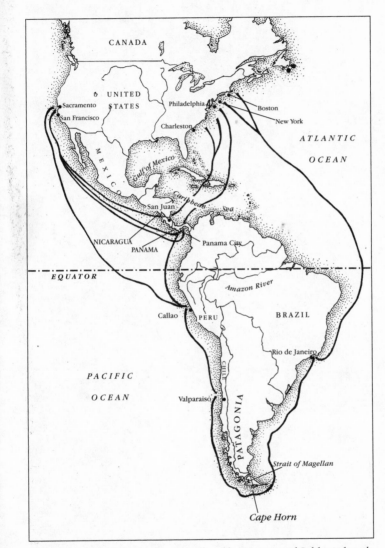

This is a map of the approximate routes to the gold-mining region of California from the east coast of the United States.

# ABOUT THE AUTHOR

*Seeds of Hope* is Kristiana Gregory's fourth title in the Dear America series. She loves to write about the historic West, especially about the people who moved there to start new lives.

When her editor asked her to write about the Gold Rush, Ms. Gregory was thrilled because California is her native state and she grew up with the lore of the Forty-niners. She decided to tell this story through the eyes of a family who just happened to be aboard the steamship *California* when it encountered the first miners heading for gold country.

"I wanted to show the pandemonium and the hopes that people had. Most everyone wanted to become rich and believed that it was possible. I also wanted to show how sometimes the dreams we have are interrupted or changed because of circumstances beyond our control.

"The Fairchilds found themselves in the midst of one of the most exciting times in American history. Despite their personal tragedy and despite Papa's gold fever, the family managed to pull together. It was strength of character that saw them through, not the money they made."

Kristiana Gregory has written two other Dear America books about the great western migration: *Across the Wide and Lonesome Prairie: The Oregon Trail Diary of Hattie Campbell*, and *The Great Railroad Race: The Diary of Libby West*. Her most recent title is *Cleopatra VII: Daughter of the Nile*, for the Royal Diaries series. This and *The Winter of Red Snow: The Revolutionary War Diary of Abigail Jane Stewart* have been made into movies for HBO.

She lives with her husband and sons in Boise, Idaho. They have two golden retrievers who do nothing but nap and wait by their bowls for dinner. In her spare time Ms. Gregory likes to read, swim, daydream, and walk those lazy dogs.

# ACKNOWLEDGMENTS

Grateful acknowledgment is made for permission to reprint the following:

Cover portrait: Detail of the painting *Jeune berger debout* by William Adolphe Bouguereau, Christie's Images, New York.

Cover background: Detail of the painting *Miners in the Sierras* by Charles Christian Nahl, Smithsonian American Art Museum, Washington, D.C./Art Resource.

Page 173 (top): Crowded steamer to California by Panama. Courtesy of Corbis-Bettman.

Page 173 (bottom): The brig *Euphemia*. Courtesy of The Society of California pioneers.

Page 174 (top): *Emigrant's Guide to California*, 1849. Courtesy of The Granger Collection, New York.

Page 174 (bottom): Portrait of Forty-niner. Courtesy of The Society of California Pioneers.

Page 175 (top): Men surrounding woman. Courtesy of Hulton Getty/Archive Photos.

Page 175 (bottom): Corset ad from Ferris Corset Co. Courtesy of National Museum of American History, Archives Center, Warshaw Collection.

Page 176 (top): Detail of the painting *Miners in the Sierras* by Charles Christian Nahl, Smithsonian American Art Museum, Washington, D.C./Art Resource.

Page 176 (bottom): Amputation kit. Courtesy of Henry Groskinsky.

Page 177: Griddle cakes recipe, public domain.

Page 178: *Clementine*, public domain.

Page 179: Map by Heather Saunders.

# OTHER BOOKS IN THE DEAR AMERICA SERIES

A Journey to the New World
The Diary of Remember Patience Whipple
*by Kathryn Lasky*

The Winter of Red Snow
The Revolutionary War Diary of Abigail Jane Stewart
*by Kristiana Gregory*

When Will This Cruel War Be Over?
The Civil War Diary of Emma Simpson
*by Barry Denenberg*

A Picture of Freedom
The Diary of Clotee, a Slave Girl
*by Patricia C. McKissack*

Across the Wide and Lonesome Prairie
The Oregon Trail Diary of Hattie Campbell
*by Kristiana Gregory*

So Far from Home
The Diary of Mary Driscoll, an Irish Mill Girl
*by Barry Denenberg*

I Thought My Soul Would Rise and Fly
The Diary of Patsy, a Freed Girl
*by Joyce Hansen*

West to a Land of Plenty
The Diary of Teresa Angelino Viscardi
*by Jim Murphy*

Dreams in the Golden Country
The Diary of Zipporah Feldman
*by Kathryn Lasky*

A Line in the Sand
The Alamo Diary of Lucinda Lawrence
*by Sherry Garland*

Standing in the Light
The Captive Diary of Catherine Carey Logan
*by Mary Pope Osborne*

Voyage on the Great *Titanic*
The Diary of Margaret Ann Brady
*by Ellen Emerson White*

My Heart Is on the Ground
The Diary of Nannie Little Rose, a Sioux Girl
*by Ann Rinaldi*

The Great Railroad Race
The Diary of Libby West
*by Kristiana Gregory*

The Girl Who Chased Away Sorrow
The Diary of Sarah Nita, a Navajo Girl
*by Ann Turner*

➜ ⬅

Copyright © 2001 by Kristiana Gregory


All rights reserved. Published by Scholastic Inc.
DEAR AMERICA®, SCHOLASTIC, and associated logos are trademarks
and/or registered trademarks of Scholastic Inc.

Library of Congress Cataloging-in-Publication Data
Kristiana, Gregory.

Seeds of hope : the gold rush diary of Susanna Fairchild, California
Territory, 1849 / by Kristiana Gregory.
p. cm. — (Dear America)
Summary: A diary account of fourteen-year-old Susanna Fairchild's
life in 1849, when her father succumbs to gold fever on the way
to establish his medical practice in Oregon after losing his wife
and money on their steamship journey from New York. Includes a
historical note.

ISBN 0-590-51157-2
1. California — Gold discoveries — Juvenile fiction. [1. California —
Gold discoveries — Fiction. 2. Gold mines and mining — Fiction.
3. Frontier and pioneer life — California — Fiction.
4. Greed — Fiction. 5. Diaries — Fiction.]
I. Title. II. Series.

PZ7.G8619 Se 2001
[Fic] — dc21          00-063725

10 9 8 7                                                    08

The display type was set in Golden Cockerel.
The text type was set in Bookman.
Book design by Elizabeth B. Parisi
Photo research by Zoe Moffitt
➜ ⬅
Printed in the U.S.A.
First edition, June 2001